FAST GIRLS

FAST GIRLS

EROTIC STORIES BY WOMEN

EDITED BY
RACHEL KRAMER BUSSEL

CLEIS
PRESS

Published in the United States by Cleis Press Inc., 2246 Sixth Street, Berkeley, California 94710.

Printed in the United States.
Cover design: Scott Idleman
Cover photograph: Scott Stulberg/Getty Images
Text design: Frank Weidemann
Cleis Press logo art: Juana Alicia
First Edition.
10 9 8 7 6 5 4 3 2 1

ISBN: 978-1-57344-384-5

Contents

INTRODUCTION: FAST IS A (SEXY) STATE OF MIND

*I like the fast girls best/they do whatever they
wanna do.*

—Sarge, "Fast Girls"

named this book after a song called "Fast Girls" by an indie
pop/rock band called Sarge.* That song is a feisty, punk-rock
ode to a hot girl who is captivating in all kinds of ways.

I'm sure you know a girl like that. Or a woman. Or a lady.
Or a butch. Or a femme. Or...you get the idea. She's the kind of
babe who takes no prisoners, who owns her life and her sexuality and not only doesn't apologize for them, makes sure you
notice her and what she's all about.

Two definitions of "fast," according to Merriam-Webster,
are "wild" or "sexually promiscuous," and while that is
the seed of what I was angling for here, I didn't just want to

*For more about Sarge, visit parasol.com/artists/sarge.asp.

read about slut after slut after slut. I wanted to read about women who in some way defy the conventional norms—whatever those are in this day and age. That doesn't mean being shocking for shock's sake but following their passion, seeking out what it is that they need to be truly pleasured. What I love about these fast girls is that even as they are bold, daring and dynamic, they have a thing or two to learn about sex and themselves.

Consider Susie Hara's fifty-one-year-old protagonist in "Waiting for Beethoven" as she gets it on with a younger man. In current pop culture terms, she's the cougar, the aggressive older woman seeking her sexy prey. But she is actually nervous and uncertain, as well as aroused. "And now there was no point in telling him she wasn't going to come when she could already feel a wave of pleasure rolling inside her, kind of a pre-coming feeling, but different than usual; she couldn't really tell what was her clit and what were the walls inside her and what was contracting and what was releasing, and then she realized she must be coming because her body had taken over and been taken over in this luscious finger symphony so she just gave in," writes Hara, in a description of female orgasm that I think will be familiar to many.

In this book, fast is as much a state of mind as a state of motion. It's not about trying to slut it up to impress anyone, but about finding what works for you. I was intrigued to find that playing with prostitution, or whoring, came up as a theme in many submissions, as did threesomes with one woman and two men. It makes sense that fast would be associated with women who mix cash and sex, as happens in Angela Caperton's "Playing the Market," where the new economy mixes with the world's oldest profession. In my "Whore Complex," whoredom is more a state of mind, a go-to fantasy that leaps from the bounds of dirty talk to real life with some unusual consequences. There's also exhibitionism, such as in Jacqueline Applebee's "Five-Minute Porn Star," and submission—there's a lot of very hot female submission and BDSM play in this book.

These girls are fast when they want to be…and slow at other times. They want to crack their lovers' secret codes, find out what makes them tick, as happens in Charlotte Stein's "Married Life." I like this story because the wife is not just passively accepting her humdrum sex life, but she doesn't want to have an affair or get a divorce. She wants her husband, the man she loves, but she wants him openly, honestly, freely, and when they both give a little of themselves and bravely bare their souls, they find true happiness.

These girls don't give it up for just anyone. Even the ones who get around have a reason for choosing their lovers, and it's those reasons, those images, that resonate with me. Here's Tristan Taormino in "Winter, Summer," rhapsodizing about the woman she's about to seduce (or perhaps, who's about to seduce her is more accurate):

She's the boy I have dreamed about and jerked off to too many times to count. The one who won't leave my fantasies, who cruises me in my bedroom, who seduced me months ago in another lifetime with her voice, who plays pool and drinks beer, who grabs my ass in crowded bars just to fuck with my boundaries and catch me off guard, who makes my brain get wet and my pussy explode.

Exactly. Though there are women on the prowl here, women who go after younger men, women who pounce, women who pursue, there are others who are excited about being the object of another's affection, lust and desire. For them, being fast means courting the man or woman (or more than one person) they are searching for.

These fast girls speak to me on many levels. I admire them, respect them, marvel at them, raise my eyebrows at them, want them. But most of all, I'm excited that they've broken free of whatever messages we all receive about how a woman is "supposed" to act, and instead they are bent on acting however they damn well please. And that's my personal definition of a fast, not to mention foxy, girl.

Rachel Kramer Bussel
New York City

TEMPTATION

Kayla Perrin

No one should be that good looking.

That was the thought I had as I watched him from my bedroom window, the muscles in his back rippling as he plunged the shovel into the moist ground, over and over again. I'd never considered watching a man do garden work a sexual experience before, but as I watched him, my body grew warm in places it hadn't been warm in a long time. I couldn't help thinking of him plunging something else into a very different moist place.

Perhaps he sensed me looking, because he looked up suddenly. I should have stepped away from the window to avoid getting caught staring but I didn't. At thirty-seven, I was entitled to peer out my window without being shy.

And I was also allowed to enjoy some eye candy.

He smiled and waved. I waved back, offering my own tentative smile.

And that's when I stepped away from the window, wondering

what the heck I was doing. *Flirting?* With a *twenty-year-old?*

Ogling was one thing. I didn't have a problem about visually appreciating his body. But flirting was...well, it was ridiculous, and would certainly lead to disappointment.

I was seventeen years his senior. Flirting with him would lead nowhere.

But still, as I made my way downstairs, I was unable to pull my thoughts from him. His name was Miguel and he was from Cancún, but he didn't speak with a Spanish accent as he'd come to Dallas when he was a couple of years old. I knew this from his parents, who lived several houses down from mine. We weren't very close, but we stopped to chat from time to time, and attended neighborhood cookouts and such less often since my husband and I had gotten divorced two years ago, but we were still friendly.

I wondered if Maria knew that the women in the neighborhood considered her son the resident hottie. He was steadily employed to do various yard work, mostly because the neighborhood women—like myself—enjoyed a little eye candy with our morning coffee.

Finished with my first cup of coffee, I strolled into the kitchen and poured myself a second. It was still early—the best time of day for a person to do any kind of yard work in Dallas in the summer, before the sun's heat became unbearable. I didn't expect Miguel to work beyond noon.

Just as I was about to add cream and sugar to my coffee, my doorbell sounded. I hurried to the door, wondering who it might be at ten o'clock on a Saturday morning.

I didn't expect to see Miguel.

He was shirtless, wearing only a pair of cutoff denim jeans. His olive-colored skin was glistening with a sheen of sweat, and I couldn't stop the racy thought that popped into my mind. I wondered what it would feel like to have that hot, slick body pressed against my own.

"Mrs. Collins," Miguel began, "I was wondering if I could have a glass of water?"

"Of course," I said. "I'm sorry. I should have offered you something." It was the first day he'd started working for me, and I'd been so obsessed with ogling him that I'd forgotten to be courteous. "I have sweet tea. Would you like some of that instead?"

"Sure. Sweet tea would be great."

I left Miguel in the foyer and hurried to the kitchen, where I poured him a tall glass of sweet tea. Less than a minute later, I was handing it to him.

He took the glass and drank the entire contents. I watched as his Adam's apple worked up and down with each swallow. Then my eyes went lower, to his muscular pecs and incredibly defined biceps. When he finished drinking, I quickly raised my eyes from his hot, hard body back to his face.

"Thank you, Mrs. Collins."

"Please—just call me Tracy. I'm not married anymore. I'm not a Mrs."

"All right. Thank you, Tracy."

Miguel handed me the empty glass, and I expected him to turn and leave. But when he didn't, I made some small talk. "How's the garden coming along?"

"It's fine. You'll have the best flower garden in the neighborhood."

"Wonderful." I liked his strong jawline. I liked his full lips. Hell—I liked a lot more than that.

Again, Miguel stood there—not speaking, not leaving.

"Did you need another drink?" I asked him.

"No." His voice was low, husky. His eyes had darkened slightly.

And the way he was looking at me... Was I wrong, or was there lust in his eyes?

"Then is there something else you need?" I asked.

"Yes." He paused. Swallowed. "Yes, definitely."

My body flushed. Something had changed between us. Something hot had sparked and we both felt it.

Miguel took a step toward me, one that was tentative but also purposeful. I drew in a sharp breath but didn't back away.

"I saw you watching me," he said.

I said nothing.

"Did you like what you saw?"

That was a loaded question, one I was surprised he was asking. "You're very attractive," I admitted. "Women like looking at attractive men."

"I like looking at you, too." Miguel's eyes swept over my body, from head to toe, leaving my skin hot. I was wearing a simple blouse and skirt, but his eyes made me feel as sexy as if I were wearing skimpy lingerie. "You're hot. The hottest woman on the block."

Hottest woman. Those words, although flattering, reminded me of our age difference, reminded me that thirty-seven-year-old women didn't flirt with twenty-year-old boys.

"Miguel, I—"

He placed a finger on my lips and shushed me. "Don't say it. Don't say I'm too young."

He had read my mind. "I'm thirty-seven."

"You're beautiful."

In other words, my age didn't matter to him. A tremor of longing rocked my body. I was trying to do the right thing—stop this flirtation before it went too far. But Miguel's words were weakening my resolve and leading me down the road of temptation.

"I'm flattered—"

"I want to leave you feeling more than flattered. Much more."

When I didn't speak, Miguel took my hand in his and raised it to his naked chest. He placed my palm over one hard pec. I liked the way my dark brown skin looked against his pale brown complexion, but what I wanted most was to feel my naked breasts pressed against his hard chest.

He moved my hand lower, down his ripped belly. Slowly. Letting my fingers appreciate the feel of his body.

"You're twenty," I said meekly, a feeble protest.

He placed my hand over his erect cock. "Does this feel like a boy's, or a man's?"

Shamelessly, I felt the length and girth of him—and a shuddery breath oozed out of me. No hint of a boy here. His cock felt strong and powerful.

And I wanted it.

Miguel suddenly pulled me into his arms, kissing me deeply, showing me just how hungry he was for me. I kissed him back, my tongue mating with his fiercely. He wasn't a boy, not at all. He was a man who knew what he wanted.

Just as I was a woman who knew what she wanted.

Easing me backward as he kissed me, Miguel led me to the nearby living room, where he tore his lips from mine only as we neared the sofa. His lips soon returned to make contact with my neck, kissing a path from the underside of my jaw, near my ear, to the hollow at my neck.

His warm hands slipped beneath my blouse, and damn, it felt so good, like an electric shock of pure pleasure.

When Miguel's hands pushed my bra away and covered my breasts, I gasped from the intense pleasure, gasped, then bit down on his shoulder blade.

In a flurry of motion, we got naked. Miguel pulled my shirt and bra over my head. I unfastened the clasp on his jeans. He got onto his knees and dragged my skirt and thong down my hips.

And then there he was, on his knees before my naked body, his face so close to my pussy that I could feel the heat of his breath on my clit. I held my own breath and looked down at him. He glanced up at me and smiled—the way he had smiled when he'd looked at me from the window.

Both of his hands went to my pussy, spreading my folds and exposing my clit. "Fuck, look at you."

I was so aroused—from his words, from the heat of his eyes, from the heat of his breath—that I almost came.

He circled the pad of his thumb over my clitoris, then slipped a finger into my moist, slick place. He groaned, a deep, lustful sound. And then he couldn't hold back, didn't hold back. He buried his face in my pussy, licking my clit, sucking it, gently grazing it with his teeth. All the while he was finger-fucking me, making me delirious with delicious sensations.

"Come in my mouth," Miguel urged me. Then he sucked on my clitoris steadily but gently, swallowing my essence and groaning with pleasure.

I looked down at him and watched his lips and tongue devouring my swollen clit. It was all I could stand. My entire body trembled as my orgasm began to build, and within seconds I was digging my fingers into Miguel's shoulders and shaking from head to toe. He swallowed my orgasm, ate me until my body went limp and I collapsed onto the sofa.

"Fuck me," I cried. "Fuck me. Please. Now."

Miguel stood, and my eyes went to his cock. The head was thick, his girth and length impressive. I wanted to ride him, wanted it more than I had wanted anything.

He took a moment to pull a condom from his jeans pocket,

unwrap it and slip it on. Then he settled between my thighs. Using his hand, he guided the head of his penis along the opening of my vagina.

I locked my legs around his hips and kissed him. His tongue entered my mouth at the same moment his cock plunged into my pussy. I cried out, the pleasure far more intense than I could have imagined. With Miguel's hard body pressed against my soft one, we fucked with the unbridled passion of two people giving in to temptation for the first time.

We came hard, my legs and arms locked around Miguel's body, his cock deep inside of me. We were drenched with sweat, and the scent of sex filled the air. The neighbors might have been wondering where Miguel had disappeared to, but I didn't care. I wanted to stay on the sofa with our bodies entwined.

I wanted more of him.

After a few minutes, Miguel eased back and stared down at me, grinning that sexy smile of his.

"I'd better get back to work," he said.

He was right. "Yes, I guess you should." But I tightened my arms around his chest, not yet ready to let him go. "But thank you. I...I needed that."

"You're welcome." He kissed me briefly.

I knew this wasn't about love, but I couldn't help thinking about what would happen next. One taste of Miguel suddenly didn't feel like enough.

That was the thought I had as he slipped back into his shorts and I got back into my clothes. Dressed again, we faced each other.

"I had a great time," I said awkwardly. I'd never done this before. I didn't know the script.

Miguel kissed my cheek softly, then whispered hotly in my ear, "Tomorrow? Same time?"

Now it was my turn to smile. "Absolutely."

"Good." Miguel winked. "This is one job I'm looking forward to."

I couldn't stop grinning as Miguel exited the house—because I kept thinking about the promise of tomorrow.

As far as I was concerned, it couldn't come fast enough.

I couldn't wait for a second, delicious taste of him.

WAXING ELOQUENT

Donna George Storey

This wasn't the way it was supposed to be. I wasn't planning to fuck anyone during the two weeks I was house-sitting at my brother's condo in Manhattan Beach. And the only hair removal on the schedule was to figure out how to yank my bearded—and very married—boyfriend out of my life for good.

Unfortunately, the plan started going wrong about an hour after my brother and his fiancée left to catch their flight to Barcelona. I was surfing on my laptop in Mike's airy kitchen when an email from my advisor, Professor Connors, popped up in my inbox.

He wanted to know if I'd arrived safely. This was a perfectly collegial question, except that he tacked on a little P.S. asking me what I was wearing. Was it that filmy dress that showed off my sweet little raspberry nipples?

I was just about to type back: *Don't forget I'm in L.A., so I'm wearing a string bikini. My thong's pressing up into my tender slit like a man's finger, and I'm so worked up, I'm juicing up my brother's chair....*

Fortunately, at the last minute I had the good sense to shut down the computer instead, but I was still trembling like a junkie. It was so fucked up, and yet I couldn't resist him. Carl Connors had taken an interest in my intellectual development from the day I started grad school last fall. The bond was purely platonic. Except when we "lost our heads."

We lost our heads in the grove behind the library—and I lost my panties somewhere in the leaves when he took me up against a tree after an evening lecture on "The Fluidity of Gender in Internet Chatrooms."

We lost our heads on the way back from a conference in San Jose after he confessed he'd never fucked a woman in the ass. We both agreed it was a necessity for his career that he grease up his cock with Vaseline from 7-11 and shoot his load in my back door in a cheap motel room that very afternoon.

That doesn't even include the day he asked me to stop by his office so he could show off the sex toys he'd collected from the woman-friendly vibrator store on San Pablo. It seemed like research at the time to let him bend me over his desk, a pink butt plug in one hole, a purple dildo in the other, while he buzzed my clit to multiple orgasms with a battery-powered silver egg. But, to be honest, afterward I felt a little used and empty.

Part of the reason I'd jumped at my brother's offer, even though I hate the L.A. beach scene, was to find my head and glue it on good.

Of course, Carl and I had decided that the cybersex part didn't really count as cheating on his wife. Our habit of exchanging sexually explicit messages was merely an extension of our common fascination with the construction of gender and eroticism in the Internet age. But here, under the relentless L.A. sun, it was painfully obvious that all my professor and I were doing was preparing for second careers as porn writers.

This vacation was definitely time for a fresh start. From now on, I'd only share my body—and my words—with a lover who could be open and honest with me and himself. I decided I should mark the occasion with a proper ritual, something very L.A. Maybe a spa purification treatment involving avocado pulp?

Suddenly an earthy female laugh roused me from my saintly musings. I glanced across the courtyard that separated Mike's house from its neighbor to see a tall, good-looking couple in beach wear groping each other outside their patio door. Actually, the slinky red-haired woman in the thong bikini was doing the grabbing. Muscle Boy was mostly trying, unsuccessfully, to fend her off.

"Come on, Cody, let me suck it here."

"Cool it, Jess, we'll be inside in a minute."

"You might be saying 'no' up there, but down here you're saying 'yes, yes, yes!'" She giggled again and I wondered if she was drunk or high.

He finally got the door unlocked and she pushed him inside, still laughing. The guy shot a quick look across the courtyard. I almost ducked, but he didn't seem to see me, because his expression was blank as he slid the glass door closed and let the redhead back him up against the wall that separated the living room from the galley kitchen.

It occurred to me that I'd merely switched perversions, from Internet sex addict to salacious voyeur, but I couldn't stop staring. The woman fell to her knees and yanked the man's swim trunks down to reveal a rather impressive baton that seemed to wave hello to its kneeling admirer. She grabbed his erection in one hand and leaned forward, her tongue extended like that of a brat on the playground. The guy looked down at her, his face shadowed, unreadable. She gave the head of his cock a few quick licks, then immediately gobbled him up in her mouth as if she were starving. Given her 100 percent fat-free figure, she probably was. That's when his head lolled back and I could see his handsome face, but the expression was strange, less ecstasy than a grimace of resignation.

It was the saddest blow job I'd ever seen.

I slipped out of my chair and crept up the stairs to the bedroom, aroused and disturbed at the same time. I remembered Mike had mentioned his new neighbor, a struggling actor who'd finally scored a supporting role in a popular series. The show was called "Family Secrets," a comedy about a gay man and his wacky family. The neighbor played the straight brother who was always falling into bed with a new woman to prove his heterosexuality. Apparently this Cody Cheyenne was now much in demand, and Mike guessed he'd be moving up the coast to a better place soon.

If the scene outside the window was any indication, the poor guy was getting sucked dry both on the job and off.

I flopped down on the bed, still reeling from the X-rated reality-TV show I'd just witnessed. Maybe this was the L.A. ritual I'd wanted, my own wake-up call to renounce pathetic, meaningless sex.

So then why was I all tingly *down there*, my mouth and fingers itching to make that pretty boy sing a different tune? Without really thinking, I slipped my hand between my legs and imagined I was on my knees sucking his strawberry-Popsicle cock, raking his muscled belly with my fingertips. All the while he moaned and babbled I was the best cocksucker ever, a veritable goddess of fellatio. Sure, I felt a little guilty diddling myself to thoughts of my brother's neighbor, but Professor Carl was always saying that celebrity fantasies were a safe way to work out our complex sexual desires. Millions of young women masturbated while dreaming about Cody Cheyenne; one more couldn't hurt anybody.

Right?

Now, one week later, I'm lying on a table in a salon in Westwood, waiting for some nice lady in a white coat to rip off all my pubic hair so I can go have a proper L.A. fuck with Cody himself. Which means it looks like my crush on Cody *is* going to hurt me—a lot—in a very tender area.

"Are you ready, Miss?"

The nice lady, who wears a name tag that reads ANYA, gestures toward the iridescent wax smeared all over my pubes. When she first spread the green goo on my bush, it was molten hot, but now it's cool and hard—and obviously ready to be yanked off.

"It will be over in a second," Anya says soothingly.

I grip the sides of the table.

"Cody, you fucker, you'd better be right about this," I start to mutter, but the words are torn from my throat by a flash of blinding pain.

"Very nice," Anya says, holding up the strip of wax, which now resembles the pelt of a hairy marine animal. "Now please open your legs a bit. We will do the inside lips."

There's more? Oh, Jesus.

I let out a whimper but dutifully part my thighs. I squeeze my eyes shut while Anya applies more burning wax to my sensitive lips down there. At least this time I know the broiling ache will gradually subside as the wax hardens. And that bone-crushing ripping sensation really does only last a few seconds. After that it only stings and throbs.

Why, oh why, am I doing this?

Suddenly Cody's handsome face rises up before me, as clear as HDTV, his perfect smile flashing a sweet promise.

*Because afterward, I'm going to fuck your smooth pussy all
night long.*

Then he runs the pointy tip of his tongue over his top lip.
Slowly.

Cody always knew how to get to me from the very start.

"Yeah? Well, fuck you, bitch."

Those were the first words Cody said in my presence,
although, to be fair, they weren't directed at me.

He was standing in the courtyard several days after I'd arrived
in L.A., glaring down at his cell phone. I was lounging on Mike's
deck with a glass of wine, watching the Pacific sunset, veils of
burnt orange, pink and lavender trailing across the sky. When I
heard the growled obscenities, I instinctively looked over. There
was Cody, wearing clothes this time, nice jeans and a stylish
black shirt.

"I didn't mean you. Sorry." He grinned up at me, then looked
away, immediately dismissing the freckled, flat-chested hippie
chick as most men here had for the past week. But then he did a
double take. "Hey, you must be Mike's sister."

I raised my wineglass toward him in a salute, suppressing a
snicker. I never thought I'd actually exchange words with my
"TV lover."

"I'm Cody. Hey, your brother's cool. Brings in my mail
when I'm on the road and stuff. You've been awfully quiet over
here."

"I'm Shannon. I'm usually invisible, at least in L.A. Nice to
meet you."

His eyes swept over me, taking in the filmy goddess gown
Carl favored, which was indeed showing off my nipples in the
evening breeze. A good actor is supposed to tell a whole story
with a fleeting expression. Cody's face was articulating, with

almost frightening eloquence, that he wanted to be sitting on the deck next to Mike's not-half-bad sister, sipping Malbec. After all, what else did he have to do tonight after his real date dumped him to go out with a producer?

Against my better instincts, I invited him up for a drink.

It was the polite thing to do. You might question my judgment, however, when we fast-forward two hours, and I'm sitting on Cody's cock, giving him explicit directions on how to bring me to orgasm. But I'm getting ahead of myself.

We started off with the usual introductions. Cody asked how I liked L.A. and admitted he still wasn't quite used to it himself, Chicago boy that he was. We talked about his series, and he politely asked what I did. To my surprise, he seemed genuinely interested.

"Wow, so what exactly does a sociology grad student study?" he asked, pouring us both more wine.

"My specialty is gender roles and media images. It's not so different from what you do, but from the other side of the equation. Hollywood puts the dreams together, sociologists take them apart. Actually, last semester I was a T.A. for a class on sex and the media."

"Yeah? Like what would I learn if I took your class?"

He leaned closer. I felt a little dizzy. Maybe it was the wine, or his scent—sea breeze and cumin mixed with some botanical hair product—or just the flicker in his brown eyes, but I suddenly wanted to charm him, too. I quickly thought back over his character's exploits on the episodes of "Family Secrets" Mike had saved on TiVo.

"Well, for example, we discuss things like the messages we get from TV shows. The more sex you have, the better. Only gorgeous people deserve sexual pleasure. A sexual encounter lasts twenty seconds because that's what fits into a script. The kids love analyzing that bullshit. They say it's the one class they find relevant to their real lives."

Cody gave me a lingering, sidelong glance. "I wish I could sign up now."

"I couldn't teach you anything. You could come give a guest lecture on the reality behind the myth."

"I don't know if your students could handle the reality." He laughed and topped off our wineglasses. "I'm not sure I can handle it myself."

"Is it that bad?"

"Nah, I shouldn't complain. I've been lucky. It's just, you know, when you get what you think you want, it's never what you really want, if that makes any sense."

"We talked about that in class, too, consumer capitalism and the endless production of desire..." Our gazes locked.

Far from impressed with my jargon, Cody seemed fondly amused.

"Hey, looks like we finished the bottle. I've got more wine at my place."

"Oh, I've reached my limit. One more and I'll pass out on your sofa."

"I'll make you coffee then. Come on, I'm enjoying our talk. It feels like I'm getting an advanced degree." He winked. I hate guys who wink, but with Cody, it worked. Or at least it gave me a nice tingle between my legs.

If it was that easy for Cody to lure me over to his place, it was even easier to get me into his bed. I was already tipsy, so when he proudly showed me the view of the ocean from his bedroom—the same as Mike's—I turned instead to his California king bed and said, "I'd love to hear the juicy tales that soundstage could tell."

Such provocative comments were always getting me in trouble

with a certain professor going through a midlife crisis, but Cody didn't bat an eye. "Is this for your research?"

"Well, actually, it would be useful to know if an L.A. fuck is different from the Chicago variety," I admitted.

Cody sat down on the bed, frowning, as if my question merited serious deliberation. "Yeah, it is different."

"How?" I sat down beside him, secretly fingering the silky designer duvet.

He cocked his head in a very fetching way. "It's hard to put into words. But you know, you really have a way of getting me thinking."

"It's hard to talk honestly about sex in our culture, in spite of a media saturated with erotic images. We discussed that paradox in class, too."

"I'll bet you're good at talking about those things."

"I'm all talk and little action, believe me."

Cody gazed at me steadily. I blushed and looked away.

That's when he leaned over and kissed me. It was a surprise at first, but before long, I was kissing him back, a slow, questioning dance of tongues. Maybe talk was overrated, after all?

He scooted back on the bed and pulled me down with him. We lay side by side, still kissing and pressing against each other tentatively, like teenagers.

"Tell me what you like," Cody whispered, his hand grazing my breast. "Talk to me. Tell me what to do."

It was strange. I could talk dirty to Carl for hours about every sexual perversion under the sun—but with Cody, who probably just wanted a simple fuck to pass the time, I suddenly felt shy.

At first, my voice quivered as I started telling him exactly what to do to my body. *Unbutton my dress. Stroke my nipples very softly. Yeah, like that.* But soon I found my rhythm. *Peel off my panties. Slide your finger over my slit. Touch my clit, yes, there.*

Now and then Cody added his own variations without any prompting—the slow circling massage of my swelling clit, the quick pinches of my nipples as my moans grew louder. All the while he was smiling, a sweet, lazy grin.

I thought about going down on him, but my memory of his grimace while the redhead serviced his dick was too fresh. Cody took advantage of the temporary silence to ask me, softly, if I wanted a finger inside.

"Actually, I prefer cocks," I blurted out.

"I think that could be arranged." His smile broadened and he pulled out a condom from his nightstand drawer. "Tell me, how do you like to do it?"

"Me on top." The first time with a guy, it was the only way I had a chance of getting off.

Yet, even when I was perched on his long, hard cock, Cody still made me talk, making no move unless I specifically directed him.

Suck my nipple.

Don't move your hips, just lie back and let me rub myself on you.

Fuck me now, I'm coming, oh, god, yes.

And so within the span of one episode of a sitcom, I found myself wrapped in Cody's arms, sated and floating in my own suspension of disbelief.

"That was great," he whispered. He seemed to mean it.

"Yeah, my first L.A. fuck."

"That wasn't L.A.," he said, his fingers wandering down to pet my still-damp pubic hair. "I'd call that a Berkeley fuck."

"Because of my bush? I hear the women down here all get Brazilians."

"Yeah, most of them do. But actually I like a little foliage."

Cody's finger slipped between my lips to tease my clit. I let my legs drop open. Were we on for episode two?

"I guess in L.A. a woman is supposed to look like Barbie with her clothes off, too."

"For your research, I probably should tell you I knew someone who said she had better orgasms when she was smooth down there. The day she had her wax, she got pretty horny."

I flashed on a scene of that willowy redhead, sprawled here on Cody's bed, her pussy all bare and pink and glistening.

"Actually I've been looking for the ultimate L.A. experience to remember my vacation by," I said. "Maybe I should get a Brazilian? Of course I have no idea where to go to get one."

Cody's penis stirred against my thigh. "I know a place over in Westwood. My friend said they have a special wax from France or something. I'm free tomorrow, so I could take you over there."

I turned and wrapped my hand around his erection. The tender skin was silky smooth. "Of course, there's no point unless I can test out my hairless pussy afterward and see if it's true."

He grabbed my ass and squeezed. "I think that could be arranged."

The sidewalk feels spongy as I walk over to the café to meet Cody. My pussy's screaming, "What the hell just happened?" but I'm not sure if it's the wax job or the fact that I stuffed my underwear in my purse and the hot air is tickling my bare privates under my skirt.

When I enter the café, Cody looks up from the *L.A. Times* entertainment section, his sunglasses tipped back on his head. Two women at a nearby table are casting glances his way and whispering.

"Mission accomplished," I say.

"Oh, yeah?" To my surprise, he seems flustered.

"Do you happen to know any hotels around here?"

Cody flips down his sunglasses and stands, leaving his latte glass on the table. "Let's go."

The women stare openly now.

"Maybe she's his publicist," I hear one say as we leave.

I wait until we're sitting in his Mini Cooper convertible to hike up my skirt and guide his hand to my flawlessly Barbie-like mons.

"Smooth as satin," he says, his voice husky. I glance over and note the bulge in his jeans.

"I hope you're right about this, Cody. It hurt like hell."

"I'll try to make it feel better." He flashes his famous smile and nods to a place called the Villa Monte. "Is budget okay or should I take you someplace fancy?"

"I don't care. It still kind of stings, but I'm just dying to be fucked."

He makes a hard right into the parking lot. After he checks in, we practically trip over each other getting through the door of our room. But this time he's the one pushing me ahead, yanking down my skirt as he sinks to his knees.

At the sight of my naked pink lips, he stares, unable to speak.

My pussy prickles under his gaze, and my eyes start to water, as if I were still on that table back at the salon. The whole scene is strangely moving—my new body, as smooth as a statue of Venus, the man of my fantasies kneeling before me to worship my feminine charms.

Cody touches his fingertip to my labia, tracing the bare groove. "Tell me what it felt like."

This time I'm ready for him. My voice comes out low and melodious, like a chant. "The wax was searingly hot at first. I had to grit my teeth to bear it."

Cody's brow furrows with sympathy, but there's a glint of lust in his eye, too.

"And the stuff was this strange green color. I felt like a perverted mermaid."

"Keep talking." Cody rises and pulls the bedspread and blanket down, leading me toward the bed.

"When the salon lady finally yanked off the wax, it was like, I don't know, a thousand fire alarms going off in my skin. I got all teary and I didn't think I could take any more, but then…"

He's between my legs now, curling his hand over my mons almost reverently. I push up into his palm, as if I'm fucking it.

"Then what?"

"I imagined your face. Floating right here between my legs. You promised you'd fuck me all night long. It helped get me through the rest."

My voice catches in my throat. Suddenly I feel very naked indeed.

His eyes search my face. Without a word, he reaches into his shirt pocket and pulls out a condom, undresses quickly and pulls me on top. As I ride him, slowly, then faster, I realize I am much more sensitive down there. It's as if my time on the salon table was a kind of rough foreplay, priming me for his cock. Cody's wiry curls chafe my tender lips, and I feel as if I'm straddling not just him, but a knife's edge—one side is pleasure, the other sweet pain. All the time his eyes are burning into me, fixed on the place where our bodies come together, then part.

The words are all inside me now, a murmur in my belly rising to a roar in my skull. *Cody Cheyenne is fucking my L.A. pussy and he loves every minute of it. Dirty dreams do come true.*

As my thrusts quicken, I actually start to believe it. I've stripped away my old life. I'm clean and new and sexy and beautiful. I can come on this gorgeous man's cock, like a favorite rerun, again and again.

Cody's hand tightens on my ass and he growls, with newfound eloquence, "God, I love to fuck your smooth, bald twat."

The words are enough. My orgasm crashes through me, the wracking contractions so fierce I flood his belly with my juices. He comes soon after, grunting, *Fuck, oh, fuck*, over and over.

The talk comes easy when we spoon together afterward.

"Thanks for keeping your promise to test me out, Cody. That was one hell of an L.A. fuck."

"Sorry, Shannon. If any promises were kept, it's not L.A."

So I still didn't quite get what I was looking for, even with a waxed pussy—which, in its own way, strikes me as very L.A. after all.

I wriggle back into him and smile as his cock twitches against my ass. "Then what about that 'fuck me all night long' part?"

He laughs and nuzzles me.

"I think that could be arranged."

FIVE-MINUTE PORN STAR

Jacqueline Applebee

I was once told that time is what stops everything from happening at once. I used to believe this take on things until I met Charlie. My boyfriend has the energy of a neutron star, and he's able to do several different things in the same instant, even when he really, really shouldn't. I've seen him speed along on his bike, have a phone conversation and simultaneously eat a container of sushi at the same time. My nerves have suffered a great deal since I met him.

"Slow down, Charlie!" is my constant refrain. "Less haste, more speed!"

Charlie usually laughed at my caution, but one time he didn't—the time when someone opened a car door right in the path of his bike. He spent the next six weeks hobbling about on crutches. Charlie's accident wasn't as serious as it could have been, but I guess the wind had been knocked out of his sails. Charlie hated having to be still—he was always a very busy man, but since the accident, he hadn't been able to do half of the

things he wanted. It wasn't long before our sex life had started
to suffer. A quick fumble, a brief kiss and that was that. I'd had
to settle for masturbating when things felt too much; the relief
of an orgasm relaxed me more than just sexually. Charlie, on
the other hand, had retreated into a world of pay-per-view porn
most nights to satisfy his needs. I'd only watched a little porno
and it wasn't all that bad, but I still knew it was no substitute
for the real thing.

"I hate this shit!" Charlie's curses woke me up one morning.
I padded to the kitchen to find him beneath the table, scrabbling
around for some loose change that lay on the floor. "Debbie,
give me a hand," he called.

"What are you doing?"

"I need bus fare," he snapped.

"Where are you off to?"

"The Science Museum. There's a lunchtime seminar that I
don't want to miss."

I shook my head. "The doctor said you should be taking it
easy, staying off your feet as much as possible."

Charlie slammed his fist on the table. "I've been taking it easy
for the past six weeks!"

I looked at him, stunned at this burst of temper; usually
Charlie was the calmest person I knew. The fact that he was
always busy had never made him any less serene.

"You can always go to the talk another time," I said, trying
to remain calm.

"No, I can't. Professor Hepworth is leaving for a tour of
Australia in two days' time. I have to see him now, unless you
want to give me airfare." Charlie was visibly shaking as he
spoke. I took a step toward him but he flinched away. My heart
was seized with a strange sharp feeling that must have shown on
my face, because Charlie breathed out long and slow.

"I'm sorry," he whispered. "Six weeks on crutches is a long time."

"I understand," I said, even if I could only guess at his frustration.

"I've written a list," he said obliquely. "All the things I want to do are down in my notepad." Charlie indicated his battered leather-bound journal that lay on the kitchen counter near the stove. "I'm not going to wait until I get back to full mobility. I want to do these things right now," he stated with determination. "Time and tide wait for no man."

I picked up his journal and sniffed the cover as I always did whenever I got my hands on it. I flipped open the first few pages that were bookmarked. My eyes glanced over a numbered list, one to twenty. I turned the page: numbers twenty-one to forty were laid out. Charlie hobbled up to me as I continued to turn the pages of his journal. The numbers kept increasing.

"Just how many items do you have on your to-do list?" I asked, still flicking through his journal.

"One hundred and thirty," Charlie stated calmly. I looked at him with shock, and then I looked back at the journal in my hands. How could anyone have so many things that he needed to do?

I peered at the items in detail. "*Visit Greenwich Observatory, should take a full day,*" I read out loud. Charlie was an amateur astronomer in what little spare time he had. At least stargazing was something he could do from home. I was glad that he could still enjoy this special pleasure since the accident.

I continued to read, grinning at some of the entries. "*Lunch at Planet Organic, take two hours including travel time.*" I giggled, feeling a little more relaxed about his silly list. However, my laughter disappeared as I saw entry thirty-eight: *Sex with Debbie, five minutes.* I turned to Charlie with wide-eyed shock evident on my face.

"You put sex with me on your to-do list?" Charlie opened his mouth to speak, but I didn't let him start. "You put aside five minutes for sex?"

"Baby..."

"Baby, bullshit! I can't believe you put sex with me on your list." I threw the journal at him, but he managed to dodge the book. I felt outraged, insulted and downright furious.

"Listen, honey." Charlie hesitantly moved closer, limping slightly on his crutches. "I just didn't want to ignore you. You mean the world to me." He stroked my back. "The light from the stars moves at an incredible rate, but it's nothing compared to the speed of my beating heart when you say you love me."

There was no way he was going to weasel out of this with sweet words. I took a breath, turning to face him fully. "Five minutes?"

"That was a mistake," he said quickly. "It should have said fifty."

"You lying toad," I hissed. "Fifty minutes of sex would probably kill you. Hell, I bet even your five minutes would put you back in the emergency room."

Charlie arched his eyebrow, leaning back slightly. "Is that a challenge?" he crooned. "Because I think you're full of hot air with that supposition." Charlie was the master of deflection. "But of course if I'm wrong..."

"I can do it," I cut in. "I can be your five-minute porn star. I'll blow your mind." I felt my cheeks grow hot and red as I straightened my blouse. "Five minutes. Starting right now."

I was burning up with rage, but somehow I felt myself becoming aroused like I'd never been before. I pushed Charlie backward until he toppled into a nearby chair. I drew on the tired-yet-addictive porn films I'd watched a long time ago. I tried to remember the things I'd seen—all the acts that had made me press REWIND over and over again. Shit! My mind had gone completely blank.

"Clock's ticking!" Charlie called out. He held up his pocket watch, a lovely timepiece that had been handed down in his family from father to son.

I looked around in desperation but I saw nothing save for the familiar domestic setting of our kitchen. A scene from a porn flick flashed up in my mind. I could do this.

"Oh, my," I said dramatically. "My husband's due back in a few minutes and I haven't done the dishes." I bit my lip suggestively, trying to get into the part of a porn actress. "I'm sure he'll spank me if it isn't all neat and tidy." I went to the sink, where a washing-up bowl sat conveniently full of suds. I leaned over, gathered a generous handful of soapy bubbles in my hand, and then I lathered them over my chest. "Look what I've done!" I exclaimed. "Now my blouse will have to come off."

Charlie sat laughing out loud as I peeled off my soaked blouse, shimmying as I moved.

"That water sure was cold. My nipples have gone all big." I pinched my tits with my thumb and forefinger, roughly squeezing and pulling on them. I arched up, shook my hair and gasped as I continued to tweak my breasts. Charlie stopped laughing. I gazed at him. His mouth hung open.

"What are you doing over there?" I asked.

"Nothing." Charlie's voice was a quiet whisper. "I just wondered if I could be of assistance, ma'am?"

Now it was my turn to giggle. Charlie loved his porno for a reason, so it shouldn't have been a surprise that he'd want to be involved in a live-action presentation.

I tried to stay in character as I hitched my skirt up a little. I straddled his lap, making sure that my tits brushed his face as I sat. He tried to kiss my nipples, but I was too fast for him.

"I'd be ever so grateful if you could help," I crooned. "I'll do anything you want if you fix my dishwasher."

Charlie looked confused for a moment. "Debbie, we don't have a dish…" He straightened a little, before continuing. "I'll sort you out, ma'am. I'm a qualified dishwasher technician."

"Thank you," I whispered against his ear. I leaned down to kiss him. His pocket watch clattered to the floor, but we both ignored it. Charlie's hand stroked my breasts. He ran the flat of his palm across each nipple until I groaned. I tore myself away when I felt a hard twitch between my legs.

"Let me show you the problem," I said breathlessly. I bent over to point at our imaginary dishwasher, whilst ensuring that my skirt was bunched around my waist. I ran a hand over the cheeks of my bottom, tapping it lightly. "I can't get it to start. I think it needs a poke." I looked up from beneath the lengths of my hair. "Have you got a big tool?"

Charlie was up off his seat in a split second, although I inwardly winced when I saw a look of pain flash across his face. He sat back on the chair.

"Just give me a moment." He took a deep breath. I counted to five, willing him to stand once more. Charlie got up, balancing himself properly on his crutches this time. He came over to where I stood, still bent over the kitchen counter with my arse sticking out. A yellow egg timer faced me, reminding me of the challenge that I had won and lost in the same instant.

"I can see your problem right here," Charlie said with a smile. His fingers wormed their way beneath the band of my knickers. When he pushed into my wet crotch, I couldn't help but start humping his fingers right away. I had missed him so much. I didn't have to pretend to make noises like a porn star when my insides quaked. Charlie wedged his knee between my legs, leaning on me somewhat to help keep him upright. I welcomed the extra weight, loved the feeling of being surrounded by his manly bulk. Time swirled around me in slow pulses as I came on Charlie's fingers.

"Yes, oh, yes," I cried like I was the feature artist in our production. "Love you."

Charlie stepped away and returned to his chair, flopping down heavily. However, the grin that lay on his face let me know that our fun wasn't over just yet.

"How can I ever repay you for fixing me up?" I asked, crouching to my knees. I crawled over to where Charlie sat. The bulge in his trousers was enticing. I ran my face over his thighs, and then I mouthed his erection through the fabric of his pants. Charlie hastily undid his fly, setting his cock free. I licked across the underside with little sweeps of my tongue. When I reached the head, I twirled over it like it was an ice-cream cone.

"That's it, baby," he said with a rough voice. "Suck it."

My mouth closed over his cock. Charlie rocked beneath me. I couldn't remember how long it had been since I'd done this, but time had no effect on some things—instinct and a love of blow jobs flooded my mind. I worked my lips up and down over his thick, hard cock, sucking, slurping and lapping until Charlie started thrusting aggressively into my mouth.

"Baby, I'm gonna…"

I didn't let him finish his sentence. Just like a real porn star, I ended our encounter with the money shot. I slid off Charlie's cock with a wet pop, angled myself, and let him shoot ribbons of come over my breasts. The warm spurts seemed to go on forever. I guess Charlie must have missed me, too.

"Oh, baby," he said, gasping. "Where did that come from?"

"You mean, you don't know?" I replied, looking down at my come-streaked body.

"No, not that," Charlie said with a bright, happy smile. "I

mean you're a natural porn star, but I've never seen that side of you before."

I wiped myself down with a kitchen towel. "You can have a repeat performance later on if you like," I said with a chuckle.

"There's no time like the present," he teased, again with the challenge in his voice, but then he looked at me with affection in his eyes. "Maybe we can schedule that in for after a little nap?"

"What about your to-do list?" I asked, pointing to where the journal lay on the floor.

"Screw that shit!" Charlie said dismissively. "I've got better things to do with my time."

I helped him to stand, and then we both went to bed.

WINTER, SUMMER

Tristan Taormino

The Provincetown I remember was a crowded summer street packed with the traffic of tourists and local characters: bawdy drag queens dressed to kill en route to their nightly performance; boys traveling in pairs or packs, fresh and frisky from tea dances and sun-drenched dykes on their way home from the beach, sweaty from sex or flag football or both. The summers I spent in P-town were boisterous, uninhibited, reckless. Each week, a new bunch of hot, flirtatious, hassle-free girls would arrive, party and leave. I could barely keep track of their first names. I steered clear of unrequited crushes and dyke drama extraordinaire; I'd rather be associated with the P-town dyke mafia who preyed on innocent Midwestern lesbians fresh off the Olivia Cruise boat. My motto was "Get close enough to get off." No closer.

In the middle of one of the coldest winters, I arrived in another Provincetown. Stores shut down, streets empty, and sky gray—it was silent, icy, still. I tried to convince myself that the quiet of winter would somehow be revitalizing. It was dark

when Alexandra picked me up at the bus station, then fed me
and dragged me out the door to a tiny bar behind a familiar,
yet uncharacteristically quiet, cabaret. As I shuffled through the
door, I scanned the small space. Once a summer townie, that
night I knew I was fresh meat—something new to look at—and
I wanted to use that to my advantage. I hoped that someone was
in the mood for the new girl in town because I was in the mood
for a good fuck. Alex and her girlfriend, Leta, were anxious to
get the lowdown on who showed up for the week's competitive
ritual they called the Tuesday Night Pool Tournament, so they
left me alone as soon as we got inside.

I decided to find a good seat at the bar. I felt sassy enough to
order my signature drink in the hopes of at least getting a smile
out of the surly bartender. "A Shirley Temple in a martini glass,
please." She raised an eyebrow, as if she remembered the only
girl in town who drank such a drink all last summer. The bar
was pretty crowded for P-town in the middle of winter, but the
selection of dykes wasn't exactly dazzling. No one caught my
eye or seemed tough enough to take me on. The most interesting
sight was the sharp pool sticks standing in a perfect row against
the wall that faced twin pool tables. I imagined what the long,
pointy sticks would feel like colliding with my backside or being
shoved roughly inside me. Watching a good but dirty game of
pool was like hot foreplay for me, and everyone knows that a
skilled pool player is an even better fuck.

I decided to concentrate on the tournament. These dykes
certainly were serious about playing pool, but I wasn't completely
mesmerized by the action on that green table until one player
stepped up to it. She captured me the moment she confidently
filled the empty red triangle with solid and striped balls. Such
precision and perfection; she knew exactly where she wanted
each ball and how close they should be to each other. I wanted

her to fill me up with the same power and gentle force. From the first time her stick collided with the shiny balls it was evident that her hands were rhythmic, generous, methodical. I could tell how strong her arms were from the power behind her shots. She carefully set up each shot, and before she was ready to shoot she made an unbelievable move.

Leaning over the table, she spread her legs by twisting her ankles and sliding her feet apart. Then she smacked the cue ball sharp and fast. As her balls ducked into the dark pockets and disappeared from the table, I watched her eyes guide them there with a concentrated deliberateness that made my clit swell. I wanted desperately to flirt without distracting her from the game that was making me so hot. Before she pummeled the eight ball in to win, through smoke bright from the light overhead, her attention moved from the table, and she glanced over her glasses and focused on me. Her look had the same force behind it as her shots.

By the time she had beaten all the regulars—including almost pounding it out in a brawl with a butch number who'd had too much to drink and scratched on her eight-ball shot—I decided to open myself for her first move. I coolly turned around on my bar stool, putting my back to the action. I leaned against the warm and sticky surface of the bar. Seconds later, another martini glass with a shiny, perfectly red cherry swimming in sparkling pink bubbles appeared on the edge of the bar in front of me. A small hand with flushed, rough skin around the knuckles and perfectly trimmed nails cradled the glass confidently. I hoped the hand was hers and turned coyly around on my bar stool to get a better look. I think I actually gasped slightly at the sight of her up close. Fuck, she was gorgeous!

She was built solidly and dressed like a boy, with her strong arms cloaked beneath a heavy plaid flannel shirt. Her hair was short, wet, blonde, slicked back. I always had a thing for blonde butches but never seemed to make it past the flirting stage with them. Her slightly nerdy and very smart-ass gold-rimmed glasses framed the most intense blue eyes I had ever seen. Then she smiled. It was over. I thought I would soak the bar stool right then and there.

"Hi. I thought you might like another," she said, pouring on the gentlemanly butch charm like the cruising pro she was.

"Thanks," I said as I reached my hand out for hers. She took my hand gently at first, then squeezed it so hard I thought I might gasp again. She released my hand and let hers drop to my thigh, which was hidden in black tights. She just lingered there.

"So, what brings you to P-town?"

"I'm visiting Alexandra and Leta. I went to school with Alex. You played well tonight. Is your game always that intense?" I got my first chance to smell her as she moved behind me, still fresh from a near-fight, breathing against the back of my neck. Could that really be Old Spice? Her hand traced my ass through my plaid parochial-school skirt. My nipples hardened and I knew they must be poking through my T-shirt. Then she pushed the skirt up and reached underneath it right there at the bar. I let her. I wanted her to pull my tights down to my knees and stick her hand inside me. She took a gulp from her beer instead.

"It really depends. Is yours?"

I had one chance to let her know just how badly I ached for her, just how crazy I got when she pawed me like that in such a public place, touched and marked my body so everyone around us knew to whom I belonged. I took a deep breath. "Uh-huh."

She took another drink of her beer and put out her cigarette. I saw the fearlessness in her smoky eyes, and I wanted her to take me home. I wanted her to take me. I didn't want to have any choice. I didn't want to have any small talk. No discussion, no negotiation, no latex, no lube. Just her inside me. Without my permission. Without my asking. Well, maybe begging. Pull me through the door and push me on the bed and get inside me where and how and when you want to. Please.

"Oh, I can't wait to mess up your lipstick. Let's go," she instructed, and she took my hand in hers again. Then she walked stridently, leading me past Alex, Leta, their friends, the woman whose head she had almost smashed in and the rest of the bar dykes. She was showing me off. I had a rush of excitement throughout my body, and it felt warm, like it was summer again. From the other side of the pool table, Alex flashed a knowing smirk at me.

When we got outside in the cold, she put her arm around me as we walked in silence. The walk was long, and the chilly air just made my nipples harder. We arrived at her apartment, and she led me upstairs to a large room with a loft dominated by a square, king-size bed. I leaned over the bed to see her reaching for something that she apparently found but kept hidden from me, smiling the toothy grin of a naughty boy with dirty thoughts and secrets and plans.

She sat me on the bed, leaned forward and planted the most incredible kiss on my lips. Her tongue probed my mouth as her hands explored what felt like every inch of my body. Her touches were precise, perfect, like the way she handled the stick and worked the balls in her pool game—she used the same methodical calculation I had witnessed earlier.

It was as if she had diligently studied my body and knew all its curves and tender spots by heart, like she knew the pool table: hands gliding, stroking, pressing until my soft flesh relaxed in warmth and wetness underneath her, ready to go into what-ever deep pocket she was pushing me. She pulled back from me and stood studying my body with her acute, extreme eyes. Her

concentration and the quietness that surrounded us were terri-
fying. Electric.

"Do you use a word when you play?" She said it with the
ease of a professional.

"Uh-huh."

"Tell me what word you'd like to use."

"Rock," I said, without a second's hesitation.

"Why 'rock'?"

I hadn't really thought about it—it just sort of slipped out
of my mouth. "Rocks are solid, but rough around the edges—
sometimes dirty, sometimes sharp, sometimes exquisite."

"Do you like to cry before or after you say your word?"

"Before."

"You like to cry when someone hits you?

I paused. "Yes...yes, I do."

"It feels good, doesn't it?"

"Uh-huh." Actually, I have a hard time crying. Getting to
that place where I bring all the walls down, open myself up for
someone else, lose control and let some fucking strong feelings
take over terrifies me. Oh, I love being a submissive, little-girl
bottom, but that doesn't mean being vulnerable is a simple task.
I know that hungry bottoms and wet pussies are easier to get
inside. Penetration isn't a boundary for me unless my true desire
is where you're headed. Having a fist in my cunt is a million
times easier and safer for me than revealing what's *really* deep
inside. Going to the edge and then over it can be a little scary but
it can also be wildly ecstatic. Crying is too revealing—it means
I've gone too far. I've let her get too close.

She terrified me in that moment when she said it like she
knew. None of my lovers had ever asked me about crying. No
one had ever made it a goal to make me cry, so no one had
ever gotten to that part of me. This was not just another warm

summer girl. She was serious. I wanted to know how she knew
about me. Where in my translucent flesh was it carved? What
about me made her ask the question, and why was I ready now
to go there with her?

"Sam?" She shakes her head sternly, seriously. I correct
myself. "Daddy."

She nods and whispers, "Good girl. Now turn around and
lean over the bed." She's had enough of questions and talking
for now. I do as she says.

She pushes my skirt up over my hips, pulls down my tights
and panties until they are around my ankles. She methodically
traces my body, as if she is preparing for some ritual. Her fingers
are smooth on my skin, except for her rough knuckles, which
add a coarse texture to her touches as she explores my ass with
the back of her hand. She takes my flesh between her fingers and
squeezes with a deliberate sense of ownership and devotion. I
anticipate and anxiously await being bound in leather restraints
or some elaborate rope work, but instead she ties me up with
one quiet breath. "I don't need to restrain you. You'll stay still
for me like a good girl, won't you?"

"Yes, Daddy."

Her first smack is quick, sharp, stinging. I feel the skin of
my ass warm beneath her palm. There are three more to follow.
She alternates from right to left: one hard and slow with lots of
power behind it, then, without time for me to recover, without
time for me to move slightly so she won't hit the exact same spot,
she comes down with three fast and vicious slaps. After each set
of four, she rubs my tender, burning flesh with the softest part of
her hand. As the beating continues, I writhe, begin to arch my
back, raise my ass to meet her harsh blows, offer myself to her.

She alternates the hitting with teasing, rubbing my hole with
her thumb, pushing into my ass-slit, sneaking just right inside

me, then leaving for another smack; my scream, her groan, *smack, smack, smack*. When my ass is tender and hot, she tells me how red it is, how good the raised welts feel under her fingers and how hard she gets when she hits me. Then she slides her belt out of the loops of her jeans. The firm leather is rough, mean, and hurts even more on my fleshy ass, already raw from her hand. I scream louder; I want to flinch but wouldn't dare.

I arch my back again, this time to drop my head down, look between my legs and catch a peek at her. With one hand she holds the menacing belt, with the other she strokes her firm dick, which stands majestically between her legs. Once I am reeling high enough from the whipping, I feel the head of her cock press against my asshole. The pressure increases, slow and sure, until she shoves her cock all the way inside me. No fingers to warm up, just her eight inches. Surprisingly, my ass opens up for her dick as if she had fucked me a dozen times before, drawing her inside me and sucking on her rod like a hungry child.

She begins by fucking me first on my stomach, slow and fully, which makes my clit hard and swollen. She holds my body down with her powerful arm, pressing into my shoulder blade with her weight. When she has had enough of tender overtures, she moves me to my hands and knees and begins to use my ass as she really wants to: fast, hard, cruel. Her rhythm is still precise and perfect, quickening as she plunges deeper inside me. I let my body be pushed forward with her thrusts and moan as my ass muscles grip her dick. She comes fast, shooting her hot liquid inside me as she groans, breathing hard. For a moment, she is absolutely still.

When her breathing slows, I sit back on her cock, taking the length inside my ass as she presses hard on my clit and cradles me in her lap. Surviving her painful smacks and then feeling her come has sent me over the edge, and I am riding her dick and her hand like the hungry, selfish, bratty bottom I am until I'm screaming at the top of my lungs. She's the boy I have dreamed about and jerked off to too many times to count. The one who won't leave my fantasies, who cruises me in my bedroom, who seduced me months ago in another lifetime with her voice, who plays pool and drinks beer, who grabs my ass in crowded bars just to fuck with my boundaries and catch me off guard, who makes my brain get wet and my pussy explode. And this was her gift to me tonight. She starts in on my ass again until I am past the place where I can possibly take another lash. The pain has become too intense, too much—but I feel alive, triumphant, a little tough. Am I? She has calculated it all and she knows where she brought me, where I am, where she's got me. She reaches up, yanks the hair at the back of my neck and smacks the side of my face. My lips are spread open. I feel that soft part of her hand against my cheek and mouth, and I burst into tears. I let go. I'm crying, real tears pouring out of my eyes as they have never done before.

She lets the tears stream down, wetting my face and her neck, in no hurry to brush them away. I smell her sweat like summer, and she holds me in warm, familiar arms. It's okay to feel the salty sting in my eyes; it's okay to need her to hold me, take care of me for a moment. Every inch of my insides aches, burns like my skin touched by hot tears. My heart races; I can't catch my breath. I can't catch hold of my emotions; I'm breaking apart into messy little pieces. But her arms are wrapped around me, and I am somewhere safe. It's as warm as winter there.

PLAYING THE MARKET

Angela Caperton

Who knew you could lose your ass in bonds?

Jessie sipped her second gin and tonic, making it last. Twenty-seven years old and until a week ago a millionaire on paper, now she had to hope the quinine would keep her healthy because she didn't even have medical insurance. How the fuck was she going to pay her rent?

Smartest girl in the office, Robert had called her—Mister Sure Thing, guaranteed 18 percent annual interest, now doing eighteen months with at least eighteen people ready to kill him when he got out, herself included in the happy ranks. She should have smelled the bullshit the minute he claimed the investments were absolutely safe, a no-brainer, and it was government guaranteed. Sure enough, somewhere at the bottom of a big stack of imaginary paper the government guaranteed something but that guarantee got lost in three or four layers of leverage that had folded up like a lowball poker hand in a game of hold 'em.

How the fuck am I going to pay my rent? she thought again

and smiled, turning at the bar to scan the big, smoky room full of tables and people. Funny thing, ever since the world went to shit, nobody paid much attention to the smoking ordinance. Jessie had never been in Waxy's before and she wondered if the crowd was typical—a little older than the places she usually went, better dressed, like the downturn hadn't hit them as hard yet.

She crossed her legs, smoothing her stockings, shoulders back, chin up, looking for the right guy. A gray-haired, fat man in a Lauren sweater tried to catch her eye but she pretended she didn't see him.

God, she felt like she was back in high school as she looked over the boys, knowing exactly what she wanted from them. She'd had standards even then and she'd prided herself on being picky until she found the right one. Tonight was no different. She knew exactly what she wanted. She wanted five hundred dollars to make her rent.

She knew Waxy's management would frown upon her new profession but Jessie knew if her plan was to succeed, she needed to be in a place where men had money. She remembered the punch line of an old joke: which one of the cheap bastards gave you a quarter? All of them.

No. It would just be this one time, one good fuck with a guy she might have slept with anyway, and she would never do this again. She just needed a stopgap.

She shifted on her stool, letting her skirt ride up just a little, not slutty but casual, and she looked down the bar to a man three stools away to her right. Not bad: midthirties; thick, dark hair; serious around his eyes, but his lips looked scrumptious.

He looked at her as if he sensed her appraisal. He moved with fluid ease to sit beside her, his smile confident and warm. "I'm Derrick," he said. "Derrick Johns."

"Jessie," she nearly purred as she broke his gaze and looked down, a little shy but not sure why. His eyes were deep blue and very direct.

He tapped the bar to attract the bartender. "You work in the district?" he asked, his voice like cognac.

"No," she lied. "I'm a stewardess."

He grinned. "No offense, but you look smart enough I figured you're a trader, and I thought you might have lost your job."

She swiveled to face him, a little shaken.

He smiled. "Drinks are on me."

They fell into easy conversation; he was funny, quick and intelligent. She liked talking to him. When he touched her hand as they worked on their third drink, she liked that, too.

As she finished the drink, he leaned close and thrilled her. "I have a room at the Alpine. Will you go back there with me?"

She found exhaling hard all of a sudden. "Sure," she said, trying for a gaze that left no mistaking her intentions, hoping for a hard and mercenary shine. "For five hundred dollars."

He laughed but she held her expression, the faintest twitch of a smile, exactly as she had rehearsed.

"You mean it?" Derrick remarked, his voice a little breathless. "I'll be damned. All right. Why not? But let's make this interesting, shall we? Five hundred cash, but you have to do whatever I say. Fair?"

She wavered and hoped her weakness didn't show. "I don't like pain," she stated flatly.

"What kind of sicko do you think I am? No, no pain. Nothing bad at all. First thing is, we go someplace else. Come on."

They left Waxy's, caught a cab, and he gave the driver an address on North Water Street. He did not seem inclined to speak and she stared out the window at the light-splashed boulevard, wondering what she had gotten herself into and if she might find a refrigerator box to live in if she had to bail out of the cab.

The bar was called La Fontaine d'Absinthe. She appraised Derrick and begged fate that he wasn't some kind of secret goth, but her concern faded as soon as they cleared the leaded-glass door. The establishment was exquisitely furnished in authentic belle époque wood, lit with flickering flames from candles and a fire inside a massive stone hearth, and rich with the scent of leather and money. Jessie reined in a giddy laugh. This was the Promised Land.

In the dim light, she saw perhaps thirty people scattered among tables and a few leaning against the bar. The murmur of conversation and laughter soothed her, and the mildest of examinations imparted the understanding that inside the bold walls, no one was a stranger for long. She knew that by the end of the evening, she'd either be welcomed back as a regular, or she'd never pass through the glass door again.

A tuxedoed waiter showed them to a table near the bar, then nodded with familiarity at Derrick, confirming Jessie's assessment that this wasn't the first time he'd been here. Derrick ordered wine and a little pang of disappointment clipped her heart. "I've never had absinthe," she told him.

"Maybe next time. Here's what we're going to do. Look around the room."

She obeyed him, her gaze passing lightly over the well-dressed men and women in the bar—far more men than women, she realized. From the way the men looked back at her, she knew this wasn't a gay place. Most of the men were older, forty all the way to geriatric, but their clothes might as well have been sewn from hundred-dollar bills, and all the women looked like they had stepped out of *Elle*.

The waiter brought the wine. Derrick gave it a casual look and nodded, so the waiter poured each of them a glass and vanished discreetly.

He took up his wineglass, tipping the bowl in an almost hypnotic rhythm. "Have you ever had two men fuck you at the same time?"

The question didn't shock her, but she took a long sip of wine to buy time before she replied. Did he want her to say yes? She'd seen porn and wondered what it might feel like but had never in her life actually thought about such a thing.

Until tonight.

"No," she said. "But I think I'd like it."

"For five hundred dollars, you'd better at least pretend to like it." An edge of controlled agitation dusted his reply and to Jessie's surprise, her pussy slicked. "I want you to pick a man in this room. A man you'd like to fuck. Any man."

She scanned the room and realized as the slow trickle of juice between her legs continued that she could fuck any of them, maybe all of them, even the nearly bald old man with deep lines of experience and excess etched into his face. Power and vitality buzzed in her blood. She had never in her life felt so alive.

"That one," she said as she discreetly pointed to a coffee-colored man with a slick mane of ebony hair flecked with gray. His cheekbones reminded Jessie of an Aztec god, and his charismatic smile and shining eyes excited her.

"All right," Derrick said, his voice unreadable. Did he approve of her choice? He stood up from the table and crossed the room to talk quietly to the stranger at the bar. The two men looked at her and then spoke more urgently for only a moment before Derrick clapped the man on the shoulder and returned to her.

"Come on. Esteban's having his car brought up." He took her by the hand and led her to the man. Esteban touched her cheek with his hand, cool and soft as the glass he had been holding. His eyes burned with intensity and lust.

Esteban drove the Saleen and Jessie rode in the front seat next to him, his hand resting on her thigh. In minutes, they slowed as they drove through an outcropping of townhouses on the lake shore. The men didn't talk and Jessie watched the city, feeling detached and a little dazzled by the lights. The excitement she had felt in the bar began to turn toward apprehension. She chided herself as her fingers stroked the door release. She was a big girl! Fucking strangers was nothing, dammit.

Esteban's flat looked like a place where no one really lived, every surface shiny and clean. The furnishings were sparse and modern; the walls breathed some ambient afro-beat. One wall of the living room, all glass, showed a view of the light-speckled lake, black and endless as the sky.

"You want a drink?" Esteban asked her, his voice tinged with an exotic accent, low and warm. He mixed her a perfect gimlet when she told him what she wanted. Derrick had a straight scotch and watched her with a little smile.

How did this start? Jessie wondered. Should she say something? She had the distinct idea that Derrick was enjoying her nervousness, and she thought it might even be turning Esteban on a little. They let her stand there, looking out at the dark majesty of the view, for almost five endless minutes, before Esteban politely cleared his throat and spoke. "Derrick says you've never had two men before." He stood very near her. She smelled musk and a hint of something sweet, like lime. "Is this true?"

She smiled at him, her voice calm even as her belly jumped. "I'm a fast learner."

He laughed and touched her breast, his fingers now warm even through her blouse and the thin satin of her bra. She wondered if her tight nipple might tear the fabric as he circled it with his finger. Esteban nodded to Derrick and Derrick began to unbutton his shirt. He wore a pale blue T-shirt underneath it that clung tightly to his pecs as he breathed. He tossed his shirt aside and peeled off the tee. Jessie's breath quickened as Esteban's right hand became more insistent on her breast, almost roughly fondling and tweaking as his left hand cupped her bottom, gathering her skirt.

Esteban smashed her lips in a feral kiss and forced his tongue between her lips, rapacious, even though she opened to him, and his hard grip on her butt clearly informed her she had left consent back in the bar. She was his now to take however he wanted her. Derrick dropped his slacks, bare beneath them, his cock already an impressive plank that stood at nearly a perfect forty-five-degree angle from his body.

Jessie remembered the first cock she had ever seen, and the second, and the third, each of them a little magical as they lengthened and thickened in appreciation and anticipation of her. This was different. Obligation and a sense of surrender colored her perception. She felt no trace of selfishness, only a desire to make this the best fuck either of the men had ever had, and, to her utter amazement and arousal, to earn her pay.

Esteban turned her to face Derrick, his hands continuing to explore her. He kept kneading her breasts as he unzipped her skirt and played at the edge of her thong. He licked her under her ear and bit her lightly on the throat, then he pushed her to Derrick. "Strip her."

She wondered if she was supposed to help him, but Derrick didn't seem to need any help. He attacked the buttons on her blouse, his hard cock bobbing between them. She couldn't help herself—she reached down and stroked him. Soft as warm silk, hard as old oak, he jerked under her touch. She wanted to make him come, eager to taste him. She wrapped her hand around the thickening shaft and began to pump.

She heard Esteban undressing behind her as Derrick peeled

her blouse down her shoulders and began to work on her bra. Her unzipped skirt slipped down her stocking-clad thighs, and she shimmied to make it fall to her ankles. She still held Derrick's cock, in love with the sensation of the pounding blood inside it. Her lips tingled at the thought of sucking him, but Derrick controlled her position. The best she could manage was the slow milking rhythm she had established with her hand.

He bared her breasts and Esteban reached around her, his touch greedy, his warm hands returning to what they apparently loved: the slow, rough mauling of her stiffened nipples. For a moment, the men pressed her between them. She felt Esteban's trousers against the bare globes of her bottom, his erection impressive and stiff, Derrick's captured cock pressing at the satin triangle that covered her pussy, his hands on her garters, losing patience.

Esteban's hand covered hers, fingers interlacing so that they held Derrick's prick together. Derrick moaned when Esteban squeezed. Someone's hand was tangled in the waistband of Jessie's thong, and she gasped as the elastic strained and a line of mild pain sliced her hip as the fabric pulled and then gave. Except for her garter and hose, she was naked between the men, entirely at their mercy.

Life surged through her, unbound.

Esteban guided the tip of Derrick's cock so that it teased the shaven lips of Jessie's slit and then he whispered, his breath hot against her ear, "Go over there and get the rest of your clothes off," motioning toward the leather sofa.

She half staggered the few paces to the seat, feeling silly that she still wore shoes but determined to keep both men's eyes on her even as Esteban busied himself with Derrick's prick, continuing to pump it. She sat on the leather and crossed her legs, letting the silk of her stockings rub in smooth friction, unfastening one snap, then another, keeping the round perfection of her thigh between the men and her pussy, teasing them with a glimpse.

Esteban watched her, grinning, his hands on Derrick's shoulders now, pushing him down to his still-covered crotch. Derrick moved, quick and sure, on the other man's belt and zipper, rolling the trousers down in a smooth movement. Esteban wore silk briefs and his cock looked enormous within them, impossibly, almost comically long.

Derrick nuzzled Esteban's erection, biting the hem of the shorts and pulling down. Jessie finished with her stockings and shoes, her gaze locked with Esteban's and, as she removed the last scrap of silk from around her waist, she deliberately parted her legs and opened herself to his gaze, aware of the wet swollen button of her clit, wanting him to fuck her with his eyes, then his hands, his mouth, his cock.

The dark man's briefs clung for a moment, caught on the tip of his nearly exposed member, and then Derrick tugged and Jessie saw what Esteban had been hiding: the longest cock she had ever seen outside porn—thin, uncircumcised, arcing upward.

Derrick licked him from base to head, bathing reverently, his hand reaching under to cup Esteban's balls as he engulfed him and began to deep-throat his impressive dick. Jessie had to admire his technique. Esteban motioned for her to rejoin them and kneel beside Derrick.

He stood over them, one hand on each of their shoulders, and she understood exactly what she was supposed to do from the hard press of his grip. They traded turns, Esteban's splendid cock between them, licking and suckling, kissing each other, tasting musk and sweetness, the flesh their bond, their common purpose. While they sucked, she handled Derrick's cock and he touched her pussy with assured strokes, not entering her, but brushing the lips and circling her clit.

Esteban's cock pulsed but he seemed to have ruthless control. His breathing quickened and his grip tightened but he did not come.

"On your back," he said to Derrick and Derrick obeyed him, lying back on the thick carpet, his cock like a mast. He nodded to Jessie. "Mount him. Slow."

This was it. She was going to put a stranger's cock inside her—for money. It seemed unreal but vital somehow, a culmination of desire and debasement, but she wasn't the one being fucked here. Not yet anyway.

She straddled Derrick, her hands exploring the muscles of his stomach and chest, her gaze meeting his, mirrors of lust and want, and she slid the open lips of her pussy along his length then settled on him, one glorious inch at a time.

Pleasure flowed through her as he filled her, just as she'd known it would. His cock wasn't the biggest she'd ever had but the thick, fine and responsive flesh enthralled her. She squeezed and he moved with her, thrusting slightly up so he went deeper than she had intended, making her gasp and scattering the edges of her control.

Business and pleasure, Jessie thought as she purred and settled. Business and pleasure, and pleasure left business in the dust.

She rode him, grinding slowly, and his arms went around her, pulling her to him, raising her ass in the air. Esteban knelt behind her. She spied a jar of lube and she knew what would happen next.

She'd never been fucked in the ass before, though she once had a lover who liked to play with her anus with his fingers and tongue.

The warm, slightly sticky lube creamed her ass as Esteban applied it. His hand wandered down to the slow piston of

Derrick's cock even while his slippery fingers parted the cheeks of her ass and stroked the rosebud of her anus. Derrick held her tightly and kept her from moving. The head of Esteban's penis nestled between her cheeks and then probed.

He entered her with a little popping sound and she hurt for a moment as she instinctually clenched, but then she relaxed and the sensation of being entirely filled overwhelmed her. She lost the ability to think.

Esteban's hands claimed her breasts again, rougher even than before, but his thrusts were tender and precise as he set the rhythm and Derrick followed.

Pinned and helpless, wrapped in strong arms above and below, she sighed as the cocks inside her became instruments of pure sensation in and out in counter rhythm. Lights flashed behind her closed eyes and with the endless slide of flesh within, she cried out with her first orgasm as Derrick began to play with her clit, rising beneath her as Esteban pulled back.

She lost count of how many times she came, her hands raking at Derrick's hips, her mouth kissing wherever she could reach, and the climaxes built one upon the other to a peak, as first Derrick and then Esteban emptied into her.

They went three rounds, the men together, and then they took turns with her, a slow fucking that seemed to last hours. The sky had pinked over the lake when they finally finished. Esteban donned a black robe and watched them dress, his smile sublime.

Jessie's pussy and ass burned with sweet pleasure, and her clothes seemed to weigh a ton against skin as thin as mist. She watched the two men talk together and Esteban handed Derrick something, but she could not see what passed between them. Esteban kissed both of them good night with genuine affection and they took a cab back to Waxy's.

In the back of the Checker, Derrick gave Jessie six one-hundred-dollar bills from a sheaf he put back in his pocket. She looked at the money, then at him.

"You earned the bonus," he said. "A good night's work for both of us."

"Both of us?" she asked, beginning to understand. Derrick wasn't her investor after all. He was her broker.

"Leverage, sweetheart. Collateral assets. We can make a lot of money together."

"Partner."

PANTHER

Suzanne V. Slate

It's Friday afternoon and I'm strolling through the galleries at the MFA, killing time until Paul gets off work. He is meeting me in a small downstairs gallery where an exhibit of works by Boston women artists is on view. At a little before five, I amble in.

Immediately, I fall under the spell of the art all around me. First, I'm nearly moved to tears by a bronze bust of a French peasant woman, a lifetime of toil and grief etched onto her face. Head bowed, eyes closed, her expression is serene and resigned. I wish I could see into her eyes.

I move on. Soon I am distracted by an elegant still life of a breakfast scene and then delighted by a self-portrait of one of the artists. She painted herself leaping out of the canvas, engaging me with her mischievous eyes, a small sly smile playing on her lips. I cannot help but smile back.

And then I see you.

You are walking down a slope or perhaps climbing down a tree. You are powerful and magnificent. Even frozen in bronze, you are sinuous and graceful. Beneath your glossy coat your muscles ripple over your strong forelegs, your neck, your taut belly, haunches and hind legs. I circle behind you and see that you are male. I imagine the sculptress examining you closely, carefully molding your tight ripe balls into the proper shape. I consider how transgressive it must have been for a woman of her time to engage so intimately and yet so publicly with the male anatomy—even though you are an animal and not a man.

I circle back to stare at you head-on. Your head is massive, jutting cheekbones sharply carved below your forehead. Most electric of all is your gaze: fierce, potent and threatening—and yet calm. Your head is lowered but you look directly up at me, and I cannot turn away. I imagine your eyes to be clear and green, rimmed in deep turquoise. You are stalking, ready to strike.

Time dissolves as I circle you. The people in the crowded gallery fade into the background, becoming colored blurs. Soon the world consists of you and me eyeing each other as I walk slowly round and round, taking you in. I'm still conscious enough of my surroundings to adopt what I hope is a serious and scholarly expression, as if I am a student of sculpture or perhaps a budding zoologist, dispassionately evaluating my subject.

But inside, it's a different story. My breath deepens and quickens as I circle you, eyeing your powerful paws, your piercing eyes, your balls. I watch you stalk your quarry.

You descend a slope and arrive at a watering hole. Most of the animals scatter in fright but she does not. Sleek and jet black, she is nearly your size but not quite as massive, a little more lithe. She is on the other side of the watering hole, seemingly unaware of you. But she knows you are there, and she knows what you want. She could easily escape, but she does not want to. She is in heat.

She turns her back on you. She stretches slowly, clawing and kneading the bark of a tree. Her movements are languid and deliberate. She yawns, revealing sharp fangs and a thick, pink tongue that curls at the tip. She arches her back and raises her rump, flicking her tail so you will catch her scent. She preens, toying with you, taking her time. She knows what is coming.

Even so, she is surprised by how quickly you pounce. She roars as you mount her and plunge your barbed cock into her. Instinctively, she bucks against you, but you pin her down, trapping her under your powerful body. You envelop her body in yours and press your head on top of hers. She soon settles down. Her forelegs sink under your weight, but she keeps her rump and tail raised high. You begin to ride her, biting the sensitive flesh at the back of her neck to hold her still. You pump rhythmically, harder and faster. Your coupling is quick, intense and soon over. You climax, jetting into her as low, guttural growls escape from both of you. Slowly, she collapses to the ground.

Hot and panting, you lie quietly a moment before jerking your barbed cock out of her. The sharp, sudden pain makes her howl. She twists her head and snaps at you, catching only air.

As soon as you move off her, she relaxes. She rolls from side to side, stretching, arching her back, spread-eagled and open to you. She playfully bats at your face with her massive paws. She purrs deeply as you lick her muzzle with your rough pink tongue. You begin to lick all the way down her outstretched body. As you bathe her body with your tongue, her glossy black pelt pulsates with heat. You mouth her belly and on down as she writhes and twists her body in pleasure, purring, tail flicking....

With a gasp, I snap out of my reverie. I'm standing before you in the gallery, panting hard, sweat dripping down the small of my back. People swirl all around us. I wonder what they have seen.

Shifting my weight slightly, I realize I am drenched. My juices saturate the thin silk of my panties. I freeze, not wanting to make any movement that might cause my nectar to trickle down my thighs or seep through my light summer skirt. I feel like I should walk away, move to a safer part of the gallery, but I am rooted to the spot. I'm afraid to move because I am so wet and afraid to stay for fear of giving myself away—if I haven't already.

People press closer, hemming me in. Inhaling sharply, I catch a whiff of my own musk. Arrows of pleasure and shame shoot through me, each feeling intensifying the other. My clit throbs, hungry for release. All I want to do is tear off my clothes so that I am as exposed as I feel. I want to lie in front of you on the gallery floor with my legs spread wide. With you watching, I want to dive back into my fantasy and bring myself to the climax that is already so very, very close.

Instead, I press my thighs together, desperate for some pressure on my clit. I grasp my museum map tightly in both hands, twisting it into a tight, sodden cylinder. As I squeeze and rub my legs against each other as much as I dare, my juices suddenly overflow my drenched panties and dampen my inner thighs. My skirt brushes against the wet spots, momentarily clinging to them. Surely I am giving myself away. I want to weep from frustration and also from embarrassment at being so aroused in public.

Without warning, Paul is standing behind me in the gallery. He wraps his strong arms around my waist, squeezing my breasts with his forearms. Underneath my thin T-shirt my breasts are naked, just as he likes them. I smell his scent and feel his warm breath on the back of my neck. In response I bow my head and bare my skin. Twin curtains of hair fall to either side of my face. I hope they shield my expression from the crowd that circles around us.

As Paul envelops me, I feel his cock through his jeans, already getting stiff, grazing against my ass through my thin skirt. Instinctively, I arch my back, tipping my ass up and pressing it hard against his cock. He leans in and kisses the back of my neck, his damp lips soft and warm on my skin as he parts them and gently bites down.

I am done for. I come on the spot, in the middle of the gallery. As I climax, I feel every contraction echo from my clit to my nipples, which stiffen and throb in answer. I envision how they look right now, deep purple-red and tight, and I wish I could bare my breasts for Paul so he could knead them in his hands. With that thought, fresh waves of juices gush out of me and course down my thighs.

I shudder in Paul's arms, struggling to remain still and quiet as I ride out my orgasm, squeezing my thighs together to intensify the pressure on my clit. He holds me tight, clearly aware that I am coming. I know he's afraid to release me for fear of exposing his own erection straining against his tight jeans. From the sound of his breathing I know he is close, so I tease him. I arch my back even more, rubbing my ass against him as hard as I can, but he resists. We stand rooted together as the waves subside, and I slowly sink back against his chest.

I allow myself to open my eyes a crack and look around. Most of the gallery-goers are lost in their own worlds, completely oblivious. But a few seem to be hovering around the edges of the room, furtively watching us, shocked and enthralled by what they have seen. Suddenly I am aware of how we must look to them: my erect nipples clearly visible through my T-shirt, my damp skirt clinging to my legs, my lover clutching me tightly, pelvis pressed firmly against my ass. After my earlier self-consciousness, I am surprised to find that I do not care. In fact, I hope everyone enjoyed the show. I breathe deeply and break into a small, sly grin.

After a few minutes, Paul and I pull apart. Turning to face him, I look up into his clear green eyes rimmed in deep turquoise. I smile sheepishly and he returns the smile. "Tell you what," he says. "Let's meet here next Friday, too. This was a great exhibition and I wouldn't mind experiencing it again." I nod. We link arms and walk slowly out of the gallery. At the door I turn back to catch your eye.

"See you next Friday," I whisper, and Paul and I head off to dinner.

COMMUNAL

Saskia Walker

I vow that I will be as decadent and liberated in my sexuality as she is.

Kirstie Jefferies made this vow while she listened to another woman reaching orgasm. She was standing outside the communal shower in her university hall of residence, transfixed. She'd been about to return to her room and come back for her shower later, but the sound was so incredibly sexy that she had been forced to stay and listen, her own sense of sexual need rising all the while. Steam billowed over the top of the shower cubicle door and with it the sound of another deeply pleasured female moan. Her entire skin prickled, her pussy instantly slick.

A moment later, she heard a male voice whispering encouragement. There were two of them in there. Who was the woman? Whoever it was hadn't wasted any time getting laid. It was the third day of the new term. Kirstie smiled to herself—this was part of what she'd come to university for, liberation of the sexual kind.

"Oh, yeah, you're so tight," the man said. "I'm almost there."

The woman gave a breathless grunt in response. The sound of it sent a shiver of need through Kirstie. Her pussy ached to have that kind of attention, and she was getting more aroused by the moment. Female laughter bubbled up inside the cubicle, and then morphed again into intense moaning.

Kirstie's body responded, identifying on a deep, innate level with the other woman's approaching orgasm. She was absurdly aroused, trapped there by her need to relate, her need to be that woman. Shifting from one foot to the other, she lifted her hair from the back of her neck, where the skin was feverishly hot. Her sex clenched repeatedly. She brushed her hands over her robe, touching her aching breasts through the fabric. Inside the cubicle the woman began to pant. She'd reached climax. It was such a turn-on that Kirstie couldn't help herself. She slipped her hand inside her robe to cup and squeeze her pussy in her hand, massaging her clit until it thrummed and slick juices spread halfway down her thighs.

Then the man let out a deep, animalistic sound, and Kirstie knew he had come as well. She worked her hand, rubbing her clit until she, too, reached orgasm. Waves of pleasure washed over her. Dropping her head back against the wall, she closed her eyes for a moment to regain her composure and then straightened her robe.

The couple eventually emerged.

Kirstie stared at the door as it opened, dying to know who they were.

It was Doug, a beefy, blond, American anthropology student. The woman he'd been ramming up against the slippery tiles was Teresa, a pretty French student with dyed red hair and tribal tattoos on both arms. The big American guy winked at Kirstie as they passed. Did they know that she could hear them? Would they guess that she was aroused and that she'd been touching herself while she listened to them? She smiled at them, admiringly. Doug looked back and grinned, and Teresa winked at her, too. Whoa, that made her even hotter.

"Hey, Kirstie," Teresa said, and left the shower door open. She had a knowing look in her eyes and a wickedly suggestive smile. "It's all yours."

Kirstie thanked her, then darted into the cubicle and drove the bolt home. The way Teresa had looked at her, almost as if she was identifying with her, made her feel even hornier. When she stepped into the shower after them she felt them even closer around her. It wasn't just *hearing* Teresa have sex and wanting to be in her place that made her so hot. There in the shower, the sounds haunted her. Looking up, she saw that the showerhead had been twisted half off the wall. She pictured the French woman with her hands wrapped around the jutting fixture, reveling in her sexual freedom, her body pivoting from it as the American worked his erect cock into her under the flowing water.

Kirstie's body burned up all over again with the idea of it. Under the powerful sluice of the water the event played over in her mind. It was with a sudden, breathless realization that she became aware of all the sex that might have gone on in the cubicle over the years, all the women who had found their way to freedom in here. She closed her eyes, almost hearing the whispered voices of the others who had been in here, touching each other, sharing the heat or stroking their own bodies under the shower. How many orgasms had happened here?

"Hundreds," she whispered to herself. Hundreds of people getting dirty while they were supposed to be getting clean. The rapidly splashing water was a burbling chuckle that only seemed to confirm her thoughts. A moan of frustration escaped her lips. Her hands closed over her breasts, and she trapped her nipples between her fingers and tugged on them. She imagined someone else doing that, maybe like Doug had been doing for Teresa. She imagined Teresa pressing her up against the slippery tiles to suck her breasts, while Doug was at her side with his fingers between her legs, toying with her swollen clit, his cock hard and eager for her touch. Swaying under the showerhead, she let the pounding water touch and stroke her like so many fingertips, echoing the intensity of her fantasy with real, physical sensation. She was closing in on another orgasm, fast.

Bracing herself against the wall, painfully aroused, she opened her legs and aimed the spray over the juncture between her thighs, where the water bounced off her tender, aroused flesh. With her free hand she opened herself up to the jets of water, reveling in the sensation. She fingered her slit faster, rubbing over her clit roughly. Her hips moved back and forth, moving with imaginary lovers who were in the shower with her, their hard, wet bodies riding against hers, her orgasm fast approaching. She shoved two fingers inside, wanked vigorously, and when voices passed by in the distance, she came, crying out with joy as she experienced a second dazzling orgasm.

For several days after, it was the shower that did it for Kirstie, that communal space with its echoes of liberated sex. Until she went to the next level, the shower became indelibly connected to her ability to climax. "Getting communal" was—to her mind—the key to getting off. Nothing like tuning in to what works for you, she figured, and she was doing exactly that, having had her eyes—and her legs—opened. And she was opening up; the more she thought about sex and used the communal shower space for masturbation, the more liberated and confident she felt in general.

I want to be like her, she silently chanted whenever she saw Teresa and whenever she went into the shower and looked at the twisted showerhead. Silencing the alarm clock in the mornings, she slipped out of bed and grabbed a towel, tying it around her chest. Out in the corridor, she made her way to the bathroom area, past the two toilet cubicles and up the step into the shower. She shut the door, sliding the metal bolt home. Her body thrummed with expectation. She dropped her towel and stepped into the square of white porcelain and tiles, her core responding to this illicit fantasy, her skin tingling with anticipation of the thrill.

Oh, yes, yes, the communal shower was working its magic already, and she was going to come. Bliss. Sweet, sweet bliss. Could it be any better than this?

James saw Kirstie flit into the bathroom as he came out of his room. He paused, his interest flaring. Usually he caught sight of her as she darted back to her room after her shower, her silky black hair all wet and clinging to her neck and shoulders, that slip of towel stuck to her damp outline. She was a small woman but perfectly packaged. He'd been attracted to her right away, that sexy smile and her nonchalant attitude. She looked as if she always had something on her mind.

Something raunchy? Maybe.

He smiled to himself as he pondered that one. There was something incredibly sexy about going into the shower after her in the mornings, that was for sure. Her scent lingered on in the steamy atmosphere that she left behind, and he got a stiffy thinking about her being in there just moments earlier, soaping her gorgeous body. In fact, he'd been working off his morning erections enjoying her lingering presence, thinking about her. Visualizing her. Feeling her presence. And it was good.

He was, however, up earlier than usual, awake and ready for an early jog before his martial arts training session—which apparently meant he had to wait outside and listen to her show-ering, with a morning erection lazily poking up against the towel he had tied around his waist.

Listening to the sound of the splashing water from outside the cubicle, he couldn't help picturing her. He had a fair idea of what she'd look like naked; he'd been studying her enough. As he leaned closer he heard a sound.

A whimper?

What was she doing in there?

He frowned and studied the door. He heard the sound again and with it came a quiet thumping. What was it? It sounded like a fist on the wall. Was she okay? Perhaps she needed help. The sound continued, accompanied again by another quiet moan.

Realization hit him.

Jesus, she's masturbating.

He'd just about processed that thought when all the blood left his brain. His cock now had a real purpose, which meant he couldn't even think about leaving and trying to walk back to his room. Inside a split second his lazy stiffy had turned into a full-on erection.

Thump.

His cock jerked in response. And that wasn't all. The cubicle door rattled each time the noise issued from inside. The worn bolt that held the door shut was visibly jolting. His eyebrows lifted. Any second now that door was going to swing wide open. Should he try to warn her? Yeah, sure. He could shout out that the door was about to open while she was in the middle of doing herself. That would be a good way to announce his presence.

James scratched his head, laughing inwardly at his predica-ment. Before he had time to think about it any more, the bolt slid completely free and the door swung open, creaking invitingly. Maybe he should have walked away, but he couldn't. Maybe he should never have leaned into the inviting space, craning his neck. But he did. And he saw her.

She had one hand up against the wall, pressed against the tiles. The other was buried between her thighs. She lifted her head, and her hair was stuck half across her face. She stared at him hungrily. Her eyes were bright, her lips parted.

He'd never forget how she looked right then.

He half expected her to scream, or at least tell him to fuck off and stop staring—because he couldn't help staring right then. No man in his right mind could help staring. But she didn't scream. Instead she laughed softly, as if at some private joke.

"The door opened, by itself," he explained.

"Oh, okay. I was just wondering if I was imagining this," she responded, playfully.

"Imagining what?"

"That." She nodded down at his erection, staring at it avidly. "I'd just been thinking about...getting a cock like that..."

After a painfully long moment in which his balls began to pound relentlessly, she returned her gaze to his. There was a shimmering glaze to her eyes and then she bit her lower lip, her face flushing. It wasn't embarrassment, he realized. It was blatant arousal. Christ, she knew what she was about.

"Can you fit me in there with you?" What did he have to lose? She could always say no.

She returned his smile and crooked her finger.

James didn't need any more encouragement than that. He dropped his towel on the floor, fumbled for the door and shoved the bolt home.

When he climbed into the tiled space, he barely noticed the warm water on his back. He was too busy admiring her, eating her up. She touched his arm, measured his bicep tentatively, and then lifted her face to his, lips parted. He kissed her, his body keen and primed, his tongue thrusting into her warm, damp mouth. She clung to him, rubbing her body up and down against his, sending him into autopilot. He couldn't wait to touch her all over. Cupping her breasts with their adorable nipples, he groaned aloud when he felt how hard they were, how wet and slippery.

When they drew apart, her eyes sparkled. She ran her hand up and down the length of his cock. He slammed his hands on the tiles either side of her. Looking down, he became mesmerized by the action of her hands. One was moving up and down against her pussy, giving him a visual display that he simply couldn't look away from. Her other hand was stroking his cock so well that he was close to coming already. Water spilled down his face, obscuring his view. He flicked his wet hair back, desperate to watch. He could see her other hand moving, fingers slicked in her pussy. He wanted to taste her. His cock reached, arcing up in her grip.

She looked so impressed that he wanted to lift her in his arms and shove his cock deep inside her, so she could *really* feel it. But he knew he should play along and let her lead, because he was well into getting the lay of the land with Ms. Kirstie here. Besides, right now she was giving him the best hand job he'd ever had. She was running her thumb over the underside of his crown as she stroked back and forth on his wet skin, making him crazy.

"You're so hard, it makes me really, really horny," she blurted, grinding onto her hand. "I'm going to come."

His balls lifted, released. Semen ribboned up the inside of her forearm as he shot his load and cursed aloud.

"Oh, fuck!" she exclaimed, rubbing herself faster. "Coming is even better when you're doing it as well."

James kissed her forehead before directing his attention

back to the show he was being given. Her mouth opened into a perfect O as she reached her peak. Her head dropped back. Her grip on his cock loosened, and then she regained control and continued to cradle him while her body shuddered. She looked so good and what amazed him most of all was that his cock was ready for more; by the look in her eyes, she was, too. He'd never before stayed hard after he'd come, but this time he had. He was about to comment on it when he heard the door creak open behind them.

In unison, they turned and stared toward the deviant door.

It swung wide open.

"Oh," Kirstie murmured, laughing softly, her hands shifting to his shoulders, her body moving closer against his.

"Dodgy lock," James commented, wondering if there was anyone out there.

Two heads popped around the corner.

"Is this a private party, or can anyone join?" It was Doug, James's American neighbor. He was wearing the widest grin and not much else. Beside him, Teresa, his raunchy French girlfriend, was also staring in at them with interest.

Had they been out there listening to what was said and all of Kirstie's lusty exclamations? If so, it had certainly caught their attention. James looked at Kirstie. There was that naughty smile of hers again. Her eyes flashed, dark and sexy.

He wouldn't ever get enough of that. Or her hand on his cock.

"Your call," he whispered, one finger stroking away the wetness from her cheek. "What do you think...can we make room?"

The idea seemed to send her into overdrive, because she closed her eyes for a moment and moaned. She clung tighter to him, which James took to be a good sign.

Then she nodded, and he noticed that she was glancing Teresa's way with a knowing smile, one that Teresa returned. Hot.

"Come on in," Kirstie said to the new arrivals. "After all," she added, "it *is* a communal shower...."

FIREWORKS

Lolita Lopez

Her body hummed with anticipation as Leland tugged gently on her hand, dragging her away from the gathered crowd to a more secluded area. They moved away from the busy pavilion where the ranch's employees and family were busy setting out their lawn chairs for the perfect spot to watch the fireworks display. This year, as Leland's new wife, Pepper had accepted the task of organizing the Fourth of July picnic from her mother-in-law. It was a passing of the torch, so to speak, between generations. She'd done her very best—and now Leland meant to reward her.

Pepper kept close to Leland's back, trusting him to guide her through the darkness. His boots crunched brittle grass. The stark whiteness of his Stetson stood out against the inky purple skyline. He radiated such heat it intensified the scent that was so uniquely him: Cedar. Leather. Sweat. She yearned to bury her nose against his neck and inhale deeply. Already her thighs clenched with need. Desire rode low and hard in her belly. All day he'd teased her with lingering kisses and touches, his hand sometimes playfully swatting her backside or resting on the curve of her waist.

Leland halted so suddenly her nose bumped his back. Turning around, he gave a soft chuckle and swept her into his arms. Pepper melted into his embrace. She loved the feeling of his big, strong arms wrapped around her shoulders. Only with this man, her lover, her husband, had she ever felt so safe and secure. Leland was everything she'd ever wanted and more.

Desperate for a taste of him, Pepper rose on tiptoes and skimmed her lips over his chin. The barest hint of stubble rasped her plump mouth. He turned into her searching lips and claimed her mouth with the most tender of kisses. She loved this side of him, the gentle and kind lover behind the rugged cowboy. Riding the pastures or working in the pens, Leland was as harsh and hard as the situation required, but with her, he shifted completely, leaving all that roughness at the door. He often surprised her with his sweetness and the little romantic gestures she'd never expected from such a man's man.

Of course, there were nights when Leland unleashed his control and was wild with her. She'd never imagined she would find such exquisite pleasure from the stinging thud of a properly applied leather strap or the kiss of a flattened palm against her backside. Her satiated body often proudly bore the marks of those nights for days. A ripple of excitement shook her core. Was tonight one of those nights?

"Wait here."

Pepper nodded and stood still as Leland moved away from her. The moonlight provided just enough glow over the private patch of grass and trees to allow her to see Leland clearly. He plucked a patchwork quilt from a wicker picnic basket and spread it out on the ground. Smiling wickedly, he held out his hand. She needed no further invite and hurried to him.

Ever so gently, Leland guided her down to the quilt. She snatched the cowboy hat from his head and set it aside. His fingers threaded through her loose hair as he pressed her back to the blanket and captured her lips. Pepper arched into him. His thick cock strained against the front of his jeans and jutted against her navel. Her sex pulsed with need. She clutched at his sides as he devoured her mouth, his tongue darting between her lips. He tasted of sugary sweet iced tea and blueberries, and she couldn't get enough.

"Leland." Her breathless whisper pierced the quiet night. In the distance, the murmur of voices and laughter could be heard. Pepper tried to remember they weren't completely out of earshot of their guests.

She shivered as his rough hand cupped her knee and slid along the curve of her bare thigh beneath the skirt of her flirty sundress. Leland nuzzled her neck and nipped lightly at a sensitive spot there. She moaned softly and pressed against his searching hand. It drifted between her thighs. Her cunt practically fluttered with anticipation. When he touched her panties, his fingers tracing her lips through the damp fabric, a mewling cry escaped her lips.

"You're so wet," Leland said, his breath tickling her ear.

"For you, Leland," Pepper replied, her pussy aching and so very hot. "Only for you."

Leland gripped the waist of her panties and tugged them down with a sharp jerk. Desperate to feel his touch, she lifted her hips. In a matter of seconds, he removed the barrier between their bodies and tossed them aside. Only vaguely did she wonder where they'd landed or how she'd find them later.

He cupped her mound and then grazed his fingernails up and down her smooth skin. She shuddered at his teasing touch.

"Your skin is so hot," he whispered.

Pepper kissed his jaw. He hadn't even gotten close to her clit yet, and already her tummy quivered with the first stirrings of an orgasm. The dry night air felt cool against her pussy, her skin slick with her cream. Leland parted her lips and brushed his thumb over her swollen clit.

"I can't wait to get my tongue on this sweet pussy."

Pepper whimpered and nipped at his earlobe. "Make me come, Leland."

Laughing softly, he gathered her close to his chest and rolled onto his back. "Ride my mouth, sugar."

Her thighs tightened as she nearly came from just the sound of his gruff voice. Pepper trembled with excitement at his naughty request. She glanced around, suddenly aware of just how easily any one of their guests might stumble upon them. What if they were discovered this way? The thought of being discovered riding her husband's face ramped up the illicit nature of their tryst. She couldn't deny him now.

Leland clasped her hips as she settled into position over his mouth. Straddling him like this, Pepper felt so incredibly open and vulnerable. She pulled the fabric of her skirt tight across her tummy, placing the excess around her lower back. She wanted to see Leland, wanted to watch him eating her cunt until she came against his talented tongue and lips.

She gripped her thighs and held her breath in anticipation of that first wondrous touch of his tongue to her pussy. His big, warm hands grasped her ass, holding her in place as he flicked the pointed tip of his tongue against her clit. Pepper inhaled sharply. It was all she could do not to cry out and grind against him. She was torn between wanting to come right then and there and wanting to draw out the experience for as long as possible, to enjoy every second of pleasurable torment.

As if reading her mind, Leland tortured her with his soft lips and probing tongue, bringing her to the brink of exploding and then backing off until she'd pulled away from the precipice. He sucked the pulsing nub between his lips and moved his tongue across it with side-to-side licks. Pepper moaned and clutched at her belly, her fingernails biting into her skin. His tongue followed her slit, outlining her clit with the slowest of circles and then drifting lower and plunging into her dripping entrance. His nose stimulated her clit as he ate her pussy. She bucked against his mouth, driven nearly insane by the dueling sensations of his tongue and nose.

"Leland!" Her tummy vibrated wildly. White-hot heat blossomed in her core. She was going to come—and hard.

He squeezed her ass and nipped playfully at her clit. "That's it, sugar. Fuck my face."

Pepper felt a little gush at his filthy words. Leland hummed appreciatively and lapped hungrily at her juices. "Love the way you taste. Want you to come in my mouth."

Whatever control she'd maintained over her body vanished. Overwhelmed with a nearly primal need, Pepper wantonly whipped her hips over Leland's mouth. His tongue seemed to be everywhere at once. His nose only added to the immense pleasure. Like a tightening coil, her orgasm built in her lower belly. Sparks rippled through her thighs and into her chest. Her breath hitched and she inhaled staccato gasps. She cupped her breasts through her dress. Her stiff nipples stabbed against the fabric. She tilted her head back and fought to breathe. Eyes closed, she concentrated on the incessant flickering of Leland's tongue.

"Leland!" Head thrown back, Pepper exploded with the most staggering rush of ecstasy she'd ever experienced. Overhead, fireworks filled the wide-open Texas sky with brilliant bursts of color. She convulsed and moaned as Leland drew out her orgasm until she thought she just might pass out from the sheer perfection of it.

She'd just barely come down from one peak when Leland moved his tongue right back to her clit and forced her into another mind-blowing explosion. Shattering into a thousand pieces, Pepper fell forward, hands planted on the cool grass, and bit her lip to keep from shrieking. Leland's fingers slid inside her juicy cunt. He showed no mercy as he thrust into her wet channel and went wild on her hyperstimulated clit with his mouth. Her body was on fire. Lust and desire and need burned through her veins. Her heart stuttered as she panted and growled, the feral sounds rushing from her lips shocking even to her ears. She didn't know how much more she could take. Could a person die from coming so perfectly and wonderfully hard?

Seemingly in tune with her thoughts, Leland slowly dialed down his sensual assault. His licking and suckling grew gentler. He carefully removed his fingers from her oozing cunt and smoothly shifted her onto the blanket. Her skirt was still bunched around her waist. Wetness streamed down her thighs. She stared up at the beautiful display of fireworks. After such an experience, Pepper could barely process a coherent thought.

Leland snuggled close and slid his arm beneath her shoulders. He sucked his fingers clean, eyelids drifting shut as if he were savoring the most delectable of nectars. He tenderly caressed her face and kissed her with so much love she thought her heart might burst. The musk of her sex clung to his lips and chin and nose. She ran her tongue over his lips, gathering her own flavor. There was something so incredibly intimate about sharing this moment.

Reveling in the afterglow, Pepper tucked her head against Leland's neck. He soothingly petted her back as they watched the breathtaking fireworks display. She knew without a doubt this orgasm would be forever etched in her mind. One day, when she was old and gray, she would remember this moment so clearly crystallized in her mind as one of the most beautiful of her life.

As the last remnants of bright blue and red faded in the sky, Leland sat up and climbed to his feet. Rather reluctantly, Pepper joined him. If only they could stay like this all night, camped out under the stars...but their duties as hosts hadn't yet ended.

Always prepared, Leland produced a hand towel from the picnic basket. She accepted it gratefully. She couldn't go back to face their guests with the evidence of their tryst pooling between her thighs. Somehow Leland managed to locate her panties. He knelt down and helped her into them. Her belly quivered when he pressed a kiss to her sex through the cotton. She ran her fingers through his short hair, wishing there was more time for her to return the favor.

Pepper stepped off the quilt and snatched up Leland's cowboy hat. He made quick work of folding the quilt and stowing it in the basket. He strode toward her, looking ever so deliciously sexy even with a picnic basket dangling from his hand. She slipped an arm around his waist and plunked his hat down on his head. Nuzzling her nose against his, she kissed him deeply. "What do you say after we see everyone off we head back to the homestead and make some fireworks of our own?"

Leland chuckled sexily and brushed his lips over hers. "Sugar, I'd say you best be prepared to spend the rest of the night screaming my name."

Pepper quaked with anticipation. Her pussy clenched with need. "Promise?"

"Always."

FLASH!

Andrea Dale

You've got to admit, no matter what else you might think about Rose McGowan, it's pretty impressive that she managed to upstage Marilyn Manson so spectacularly.

Remember that dress? It was a celebrity photographer's wet dream: sparkly and completely sheer in the front, just bits of string, really, in the back, and underneath it all nothing more than the tiniest of G-strings.

Even if you're not into girls, it had to make you a little hot. Be honest with me.

And remember that time Tara Reid's dress fell down? It gives me shivers just to think about it.

I became an L.A. photographer because of the money, and because I was decent with a camera. Despite using the high school darkroom for make-out sessions with Billy MacKenzie, I still got an A in photography.

Plus, there's the thrill of the chase. I'm still young, I can run in high heels, I can bat my eyelashes and, most of the time, get into places where I'm not supposed to be.

Despite what you may think, I'm not one of the evil paparazzi. I have my standards. I don't trespass on personal property, I don't give chase if it will cut someone off or cause any danger, and I don't take pictures of celebs' kids unless I've been given express permission.

Anyway, back to the flashing of breasts for the flashing of flashbulbs. Oh, lots of actresses go topless for magazine shoots and whatnot, and then there are the ones (coughCourtneyLove-cough) who make a regular habit of showing something. That's not what I'm talking about. I mean the unintended, accidental exposure. That's what really gets me excited, workwise.

And otherwise.

The dusky patch of a nipple beneath a top that's more sheer than the actress thought (or did she?). An inelegant exit from a car resulting in a nice shot up a too-short skirt that reveals an ill-thought-out choice of underwear.

Actors are more difficult. For one thing, there're fewer naughty bits that can be exposed. I mean, who gives a flying hoohah about a guy's chest, from a shock perspective? For another thing, it takes a lot more effort to accidentally bare your cock for everyone to see. The best we can usually get with actors is a nice juicy butt shot.

But overall, it's fun. There are the outright embarrassing mistakes, the prim actresses who end up shedding all when they think nobody can see (love those Caribbean resorts!); the closet (and no-so-closet) exhibitionists and everything in between. Half the fun is trying to figure out into which category a new starlet will fall.

Take Sandrine Moss. She has a redhead's fair skin, so during the day she stays pretty covered up. At night, she often dares the strapless look, but as near as I can tell, she (or her dresser) is a master of the double-sided fashion tape, so she seems to fall into the not-an-exhibitionist grouping.

Which made her all the more challenging. A shot of private Sandrine Moss flesh would garner a pretty penny, not to mention amuse me for days, weeks, even. God knows I love a challenge.

A careful amount of sweet talking and eyelash batting (and, okay, maybe a hint of cleavage) garnered me one of the prized invitations to be on set for the filming of Sandrine's latest movie, some Roman historical love story blockbuster thingie. A limited number of photographers were allowed for one day, and most were employed by the big mags: *Us Weekly, Hollywood Reporter, Premiere,* that sort of thing. There were only a couple of freelancers, and I was one of them, baby.

One of the others was Tad, who I knew from my *Celebrity Skin* days—cute guy, with sharp blue eyes and brown hair always flopping into his eyes. (I kept my own blonde locks, if you could call 'em that, short and spiky. Not just fashionable, it kept my hair out of my way. The shot's the most important thing, you know.)

Tad had a charming bad-boy thing going for him, so he was able to sweet-talk himself into places I couldn't, and vice versa. It just depended on the proclivities of who you were sweet-talking. He and I had a rivalry going, ever since he'd been in the right place at the right time for a Mariah Carey nipple shot and I'd one-upped him with a Jessica Simpson.

Filming was taking place at the newly reopened Getty Villa, a recreated Roman villa built by, duh, Getty. It was now a museum housing all the antiquities in the collection (the modern stuff went to the new Getty Center). So it was perfect for filming a Roman-era movie.

Today they were working by the two-hundred-foot-long reflecting pool. We photogs were relegated to a second-story balcony, looking down at the tiled pool, which glittered turquoise under the sun. Surrounding it were trees, shrubs and the occasional statue. I amused myself between takes by snapping shots of one of the bronzes, because from this angle I was taking pictures of a bare boy's butt.

What I *really* wanted was for Sandrine's toga to slip. Just a little. Just enough.

It wasn't too much to ask, do you think?

It was a hot day, with the California sun beating down—and, of course, we faced west, with the sun in our eyes. The balcony provided no cover, no overhang. The eleven of us reveled in the occasional, stingy breeze off the ocean, which we could see through the haze of heat-shimmered air. The water, sparkling turquoise like the reflecting pool below, taunted us.

The director called a break and we all took a deep breath. I blame the sun for frying my brain and causing what happened next. I set my camera down on the railing and grabbed a bottle of water out of the little cooler I'd brought with me (mostly to store my film in).

When I turned back, something slipped, all right. Unfortunately, it wasn't Sandrine's toga.

Tad, bless his heart, made a heroic lunge and somehow snagged the edge of my camera strap with his fingertips, saving it from certain doom on the walkway below. Or even more certain doom in the boxwood.

I babbled my thanks and thrust the water bottle at him, because he's a guy and didn't plan ahead to bring water and I figured it was worth its weight in gold.

But he just smiled, shook his head slightly and took a step back when I reached for my camera.

"Jesus, Tad, come on. We're all pros here."

"That we are," he agreed, leaning against the railing and

holding my camera against his chest. He wore a khaki photographer's shirt, the kind with all the pockets. "We're all pros, and we're all after the same thing. You and I are in direct competition. It might come down to who gets a call in to Perez Hilton first."

I resisted the urge to throw the water bottle at his head, despite the satisfying thump it would make.

Instead, I popped off the cap and took a long drink. "Okay," I said, feeling marginally more reasonable. "What'll it take? Do I need to cover for you so you can sneak down to Sandrine's trailer?"

His dark eyes flashed with mischief. "I was thinking of something a little more personal."

He refused to explain any more until we were down in the East Garden, a small, walled plot that housed two fountains, one in the center and one, richly mosaicked, on the outside wall. It was cooler here, a bit more in the shadows thanks to the sycamore and laurel trees, and the enclosed space and the splashing water gave the sense that the temperature had dropped a few blissful degrees.

"Let's play," he said. I started to object, but he added, "It'll be at least an hour before they start filming again. We're not going to miss anything. Here's the deal: I take some fun pictures of you, and you get your camera back."

"I may not be Pam Anderson," I said, "but I know how fast pictures get on the Internet. So, no way, no how."

He held up both hands like a negotiator in a hostage situation. "Look, I'll even take the pictures with your own camera," he said. Without taking his eyes off me, he sidled sideways and set his camera down on one of the marble benches.

I suppose I could've tried to make a break for it, snatching his camera as I went, but what were we, twelve?

And, in all honesty, the whole idea was getting me pretty hot.

"What do you mean by 'fun?'" I asked.

Turns out Tad was just as turned on by the accidental nipple flash as I was. He wasn't asking me to get naked, just to flirt with the camera and see where it took us.

I'm more comfortable behind the lens, but right now, he was behind my camera. I knew, deep down, that if I put my foot down and called it quits, the game would be over.

Dangling my white blouse seductively over one shoulder, I knew I didn't want it to be over.

Besides the blouse, I wore a strappy red tank top and khaki pants with as many pockets as Tad's shirt. Not a red-carpet kind of sexy, but apparently it worked for Tad. And I knew I wasn't too bad in the looks department. I was small enough that I didn't always have to wear a bra—today's tank provided enough support since I didn't have to run anywhere. Slim waist, curvy hips, longish legs: I was no movie star but no dog, either.

I ran a hand through my hair, lounged against the edge of the fountain and pouted for the camera, baby.

My tossing the blouse away wasn't enough for Tad. Before I realized his intentions, he'd scooped a hand into the fountain and splashed my chest with water.

"Hey!" Even as I protested, I appreciated the cooling effect. I went to splash him back, remembered he was holding my camera and stopped.

"Oh, *yeah*," Tad breathed, eyes glued to my chest.

I looked down. The water had darkened the tank top, making it not quite sheer. My nipples had sprung to attention, pouting hard against the clinging material.

They weren't just hard from the water, either.

The hell with it.

I kicked off my Birkenstocks and dropped trou before Tad knew what hit him. I posed facedown on the fountain, my red satin panties (now very damp) and red top (now hiked up a bit) revealing the tattoo at the base of my spine.

Tad seemed to forget he was taking pictures. He stepped closer, his eyes scanning the Old English lettering: THAT IS THE BEST PART OF BEAUTY, WHICH A PICTURE CANNOT EXPRESS.

"Francis Bacon," I said, arching my neck to watch him. "Are you taking pictures or not?"

He squeezed off a few shots, and then I rolled over and mostly pulled the tank up, giving him some very sexy shots of the underside curve of my breasts.

"Jesus, Michelle." Tad's voice ended in a groan.

"Isn't this what you wanted?" I teased. "Mr. Voyeur. See if you can keep from dropping my camera when I do *this*."

I trailed my fingers down my belly and snaked them into my panties.

I lost any awareness of whether he was actually taking pictures. I was vaguely aware, still, of the splashing water, the heat, the salty taste of sweat on my upper lip. I can't say I lost awareness of Tad, though—his gaze on me like a palpable caress.

And I was very, very aware of the incredible slickness between my legs, and of the throbbing need to slip my fingers along my swollen clit.

It wasn't because I hadn't gotten any in a while. No, it was very clearly the blue-hot gaze of the man watching me, and the thought—the hope—that he was taking pictures of my tensed body, that sent me over the edge.

Watch me, with my nipples drilling against my shirt and my hand buried in my panties. Watch me play with myself.

Watch me come.

My back arched and my thighs trembled as my stroking

fingers and the watching eyes made me come, and come again.

By the time I recovered, pushing myself up on the fountain's edge, Tad had his hand wrapped around his cock, poking out from the fly of his jeans.

I found my khakis, found the little bottle of sunscreen in one of the many pockets. The scent of sunscreen is a turn-on for everybody, right? We've all done it with sunscreen filling our senses.

I coated my hand and helped him along. He abandoned his own work to let me do mine and I slid my fist along him, adding a twist right at the head, my thumb massaging the sensitive underside.

"Jesus, Michelle," he said again, just as his cock twitched and spasmed in my hand as he came.

I brought myself off again in the darkroom I'd set up in my spare bathroom, waiting for the pictures to develop—just from the memory of being exposed. I'd shown neither full breast nor crotch, but as the images appeared, I saw that I'd shown more than that.

The tense muscles in my thighs. The bulge of my hand deep in my panties. The naked, exposed look on my face.

I called Tad and invited him over.

I strewed the prints over the gold brocade bedspread. I imagined us sprawled there, looking at them...getting hotter...peeling each other's clothes off...

Then I went to the closet and set up a hidden camera.

To give us something to watch later, you know?

WAITING FOR BEETHOVEN

Susie Hara

S hirin is sitting naked on the terrace in the moonlight. There's
a soft breeze. She balances the glass of wine lightly on her
thigh and closes her eyes as she listens to him play. The strains of
the piano filter out through the French doors. He is improvising,
a tumbled, sweet melody. She can't see him but she can feel him,
the heat moving from his fingers to the keys, through the piano
and the floorboards and out to the terrace, into her ears and
curling around the back of her head and then around the front
to her throat and down her arms and breasts and torso and hips
and buttocks and legs to her toes and then back up between her
legs. Where it comes to rest.

It was Daniel's hands that she first noticed. She had seen him
around at work for months, but she had never noticed him, not
really, not until that day they ended up sitting next to each other
in a meeting. She looked over and saw them—his hands, placed
in front of him on the table. His fingers were long and tapered,
sensitive—the hands of a pianist, she thought idly, imagining

his fingers on the keys and then delicately stroking her throat, coming down to circle her breasts in ever smaller concentric circles until they came to rest on her nipples. She shivered, just slightly, but no one noticed. Then, the thought came tumbling in—*This is absurd, I'm old enough to be his mother.*

She should have known that telling him, a few days later, at the water cooler, that she'd been writing stories would lead to him asking, "What about?" and that telling him she was writing erotica would lead to him wanting to read it.

"I don't know. I don't think it's appropriate for me to show you a sexy story," Shirin said, standing in Daniel's cubicle last week, her voice soft and low so no one could overhear them.

"*Appropriate?*" he snorted. His put his feet up on his desk and leaned way back in his swivel chair, as far as he could go without falling over. "What's 'appropriate'?"

"Because we work together and...I guess I don't want you to think I'm—you know." *And besides, I'm too old for you,* she thought, *and you're...*you might be *too young for me. Maybe.*

The next day, she got an email from him at 10:26 a.m.

Shirin,

I certainly don't judge you for writing erotic litera-ture. Just the opposite, I think it's cool. And isn't it, at the core, a passionate expression of emotion that you're conveying to an audience? I feel that way about music, so how about this? I'll trade you piano pieces for your story. Would you like to have lunch with me Saturday and we can hang out at my place afterward and I'll play for you?

Daniel

Oh, my god, she thought. *What a turn-on. I'll probably come
just listening to him play.*
She wrote back immediately.

> D,
>
> Sounds great. What pieces are you working on these
> days?
>
> S

At 10:32 a.m., he wrote:

> Some Debussy and Chopin, but the really challenging
> piece I'm working on is Beethoven's Sonata #8, *Pathé-
> tique*, do you know it?

Pathétique, she thought. *My favorite sonata. To hear him
play it would be so awesome. Great, I sound like Cintra now.
"Awesome." God, he's only five years older than my daughter.
Is this just too kinky? I don't care. I'm twenty years older than
him. Does he know that? Does he know how old I am?*

She was early for their lunch date. She was always early for
appointments. It was so annoying—she couldn't seem to get
anywhere late like everyone else did, or even just on time. She
stood outside the restaurant, wondering what the hell she was
doing there anyway. He was late, naturally.
She saw him rushing up the block to meet her. "Hi, I'm really
sorry, I couldn't find parking, there was no place to park," he
said, out of breath. He looked distracted and not terribly excited
to see her. She, meanwhile, was more excited to see him than she

wanted to admit. As she'd gotten ready for their lunch date, she had changed her outfit three times, finally settling on jeans and a slightly see-through pale blue blouse made out of some gauzy material, with an underlayer that had sparkly squares showing through the gauze. It looked great on her but, she now realized, was itchy. *Damn.*

"So—how's your job going?" he said.

"Oh, fine. Fine. How's yours going?"

"Fine."

Neither of them spoke.

"So...how did you get into writing erotica?" he said, while they waited for the food to arrive.

"It just sort of happened. I started writing short stories and then the stories turned out to be erotic, so then I did some research. I read a bunch of erotica—actually, my friend James says if you're going to do research there's nothing better than firsthand experience—but anyway," she said. *I'm babbling,* she thought, and laughed. "Trust a gay man to come up with the best sexual research strategy."

"Oh," he said. "That's—uh. Yeah."

Their food arrived. She picked at her salad. He was plowing his way methodically through a Reuben sandwich. *Why am I doing this?* she thought. *Am I an aging fool, hanging on with all my might to my youngish looks and attitude? Clearly, he just wants to be "friends." I don't want to be "friends." I want to be "lovers." Whatever that means.* So when he mentioned something about how he had recently developed an interest in antiques, it just popped out: "Most things do get better with age," she said, and gave him her wickedest grin.

"You're not *that* old," he said, smiling.

"Oh, yes, I *am* that old. What do you think? How old am I?"

"Thirty-eight or -nine. No more than forty, definitely."

"Right." She looked him square in the eye. "I'm fifty-one."

They both laughed. He looked surprised but undaunted. *At least we got that out there on the table*, she thought. The whole Oedipal thing—well, maybe not really Oedipal, but probably at some level there was a weird mother-son dynamic. But then again she wasn't going to get into that with him, no, uh-uh.

Getting the age difference out there and laughing about it somehow broke the ice—and paved the way for revelations of past heartbreak, and then they were on to the roots of things, childhood wounds and dysfunctional families of origin. It was a long lunch.

His apartment consisted of one large room, with his whole life right there—music room, bedroom, living room and study. But the tall ceilings and graceful architecture from another era made it seem spacious. The French doors opened out onto a beautiful terrace, surrounded by greenery tall enough to make it completely private. She looked out onto the terrace and saw the single white lounging chair and had the strangest feeling, like she'd been here before. She could almost see herself sitting there, naked.

She sat on the couch and listened to him play *Clair de Lune*, and then a Chopin piece, and they were lovely, but she was waiting. Waiting for Beethoven. *Sounds like the title of a story*, she thought: *"Waiting for Beethoven."* Finally he began the first movement of *Pathétique*. She slid off the couch and lay down on the carpet next to the piano leg. She closed her eyes. She could hear him but not see him.

The music surprised her. So many years had gone by since she'd heard it. She remembered it as intense but somehow intense in a thought-provoking, intellectual sense. Now the music pulled her suddenly into its agitated world and proceeded to toss her about. She felt caught in the undertow, dragged down too far into all that was lodged in and around her heart. She didn't want to feel those things, not right now. But the voice of the music was insistent, railing against the injustice of *all this shit*, and then relenting at times, allowing for the possibility of peacefulness, and then raging once again. But unlike the palette of her mundane existence, the banal indignities of living that she had been *subject to*, the colors of the music were elevated—blue in the flame, bloody crimson, searing yellow. The pounding sounds of the piano came into her with an aggressive, relentless insistence.

It was quiet. The first movement was over. Should she say something? Was he going to play the second? She was listening to the thick, rich silence. Savoring it.

He placed his fingers on the keys and started the second movement.

The strolling melody washed over her and surprised her with its lyrical, slow reassurance. Could it be possible to have this kind of peace after the turmoil of the first? It sounded so innocent, so full of promise and terrible hope; the harmonic resolve that all the terror and pleasure and sorrow could rest together. Not go away, not be banished, but coexist in some kind of perfect universe. And it went on, with a lightness of spirit that was incomprehensible. She could feel the tears welling up and fought them back. *I am* not *crying, not now.* And then it came back to her—of course. Her recent resolve, after so many years, to make room in her heart not only for all the pain and awful smelly torments of living, but for the joys and pleasures as well. She stopped holding back. She let the tears come down, with all their cleansing grace. This is what music is *for.*

He finished playing. And again there was lush silence. She drank it in, she was thirsty for it, treasured the quiet before the next movement.

He leaned over and saw her sitting on the carpet.

"That was so beautiful," she whispered.

"I haven't learned the third movement yet," he said.

"That's okay."

She sat up. He came and sat down beside her on the carpet and traced his fingers down the path of her half-dried tears.

"I'm embarrassed," she said. "That I cried."

"No, it's—it's good."

"It is?"

"Crying is good."

"Oh."

She looked at him. He was sweating. Time seemed to slow, and the air in the room had a fuzzy, liquid quality. She wanted to swim through the palpable air and touch his face, his hands. She hesitated.

"I want to read your story," he said.

"Are you sure?" She wanted him to read it, but she somehow couldn't bring herself to hand it over.

"Yes. I've been thinking about it." He's been *thinking* about it? As in fantasizing about it? Good.

Shirin fished the story out of her bag, took a deep breath and handed it to him.

He read the story with singular concentration. She noticed that he went back and read the middle section very carefully. The cunnilingus part. Then he put the pages down.

"Why did you end the story that way?" he asked.

"That's just the story. That's just what happened."

They were still sitting on the carpet near the piano leg. A slight smile curved around the edges of his full mouth. She looked at the beads of sweat on his upper lip. *Can I kiss him? Will he kiss me? Am I imagining this? Is it hot in here?*

"Wanna do some research?" he said.

Suddenly they were down on the carpet, in the small space between the piano leg and the side of the bed, their tongues in each other's mouths, his hand on her breast. *This is happening too fast*, she thought. In a heartbeat, he had her bra pulled down and his mouth on her nipple and part of her was coolly observing everything, but part of her was slipping into a vat of warm soapy water, very wet. His body felt so hard and muscular, not like her ex-husband's, or any of her lovers who were *her age*; his body was like a young tree, with a firm trunk and lots of branches covered with green fur.

"Let's just touch and lick each other and not fuck," she said.

He scooped her up and laid her carefully down on the bed.

"I'm going to do you just like in the story," he said.

She looked at him quietly. It was like a dream. He knew her fantasy already. She closed her eyes and felt one hand cupping her sacrum. *Sacred,* she thought. *Sacred sacrum.* His mouth and his other hand lavished attention on her nipples, flicking, sucking, pulling and twisting while the delirious tickling humming traveled from her nipples down to her clit and back up again. He stayed there for a good long time, until she almost couldn't stand it, but then she felt him making his way down to her sex and she sighed in affirmation as he began his slow, lazy licking. It was then that she began to have thoughts. Too many thoughts. She was too observant, she was too in her head, she was never going to be able to come, and she was just about to say to him, "You know, I usually don't come with someone the first time," when she felt his finger inside her. Or his fingers. What was happening? This part was not in the story. What was he doing?

He continued playing her with his tongue and a digital mastery that made her lose track of time and space. She couldn't tell what he was doing but it didn't matter. And now there was no point in telling him she wasn't going to come when she could already feel a wave of pleasure rolling inside her, kind of a pre-coming feeling, but different than usual; she couldn't really tell what was her clit and what were the walls inside her and what was contracting and what was releasing, and then she realized she must be coming because her body had taken over and been taken over in this luscious finger symphony so she just gave in. Gave in. She could hear herself making a lot of noise, in the distance.

As she sits on the terrace, the cool tiles beneath her feet, she feels the imprint of his fingers, the place they have carved inside her from the last hours of love. And now his fingers, all covered with her come, are making love to the keys with the same fervor.

He finishes playing. She listens to the luscious silence once again. She goes inside. He is sitting at the piano, staring at his hands. She comes up behind him and rubs her sex against his bare back. He turns around. She straddles him on the bench, feeling the hard, polished wood under her shins. The ghost of the music hangs in the air. He puts his hands on her buttocks and lifts her onto his cock.

"You're still wet."

"You're still hard."

He leans back and the keys respond with a jarring chord. She moves on top of him. But her shins are getting sore.

"I don't know if this is working," she whispers.

He keeps her legs wrapped around his waist and stands up. Effortlessly. *Fuck, he's strong*, she thinks, in the part of her brain that can still make observations. He pushes into her hard. She cries out. She is less in control than she thought. The bench falls over. He lays her down next to the foot pedals. He stands up and looks down at her.

"What are you doing?" she says.

"Looking at you."

She grabs his foot. "Come down here."

"No."

He lifts his other foot and gently puts his big toe inside her labia, moving it in minute circles. She moans and bites his ankle.

"Woof, woof," she says.

He lowers himself onto her and puts his cock inside her again. She thrusts her hips up to meet him and when she comes down her buttocks hit the foot pedals. The rhythm of their fucking is mirrored by the clunk-clunk of the pedals.

"This is hurting my butt, let's move over," she says.

He moves them away from the foot pedals and softly wraps his mouth around her lower lip.

"I'm going to fuck you just like in the story," he whispers once again.

She moans. She tries to kiss him back but he moves his head back, then teases her again with another soft kiss on the periphery of her lips. He is still inside her, hard. She tries to move her hips but he stops her. They are completely still except for his teasing, torturous kisses.

She flashes through the images and sensations from the afternoon, the caressing and massaging and licking and orgasms and Beethoven, and into the night, the moonlight coming in the French doors and falling across the piano and their bodies and the toppled-over bench. He has remained true to the heart of her story, with minor variations on plotline, pacing, character and nuance. But will he continue to play along with her until the very end? Can she trust him to do that? For the moment? The long, stretched-out moment?

"You're going to play me then? Just like in the story?"

"Yes," he says, carrying her out to the terrace and laying her down on the cool, smooth tiles. "Just like in the story."

He slides into her slowly. And takes up at the very paragraph where they left off.

CONFESSIONS OF A KINKY SHOPAHOLIC

Jennifer Peters

I was flipping through the paper, trying to find out what the latest city council scandal was, when an article in the metro section caught my eye. The headline read, *Local Businesswomen Hope Sex Sells,* and it showed a picture of two thirtysomething women standing in front of a store located not far from my apartment. I couldn't resist reading further, and in the process I learned that the women were opening an adult toy store along my usual bus route. There was a grand opening planned for the following Saturday and it sounded like a good time, so I marked it in my calendar.

When Saturday finally rolled around, I was more than ready for the shop's opening. My favorite vibrator had died earlier in the week, and while I still had plenty more to play with, I couldn't help using it as an excuse to stock up on some new toys. So off to the store I went to replenish my toy chest.

After more than an hour perusing the shelves of the small but well-supplied store, I was ready to shop, and by the time I was done, my wallet was empty and I had a huge shopping bag full of all the latest sex toys. *Now to go home and test them out*, I thought as I left the store.

I still had a twenty-minute bus ride ahead of me, so I grabbed a magazine at the newsstand and tried to take my mind off the bag of toys next to me. It would do no good to get all fired up and have to wait to play. As I stood waiting for the bus, trying very hard to focus only on the celebrity gossip in my magazine, a line of people formed behind me. From the corner of my eye, I could see a few people looking at the bright shopping bag between my feet; some of them seemed to know exactly what I was hiding in the hot-pink paper tote.

When the bus finally came, I took a seat in the back and dropped my bag into the seat next to me to keep the aisle clear—and to keep strangers from trying to peek at my purchases. A few stops in, a few more people boarded, and one of them sat down in the empty seat next to my bag. He was attractive, with messy hair and his shirtsleeves sloppily rolled up. His jeans were ripped and he had grungy flip-flops on his feet, but it all came together to make him look sophisticated and sexy, and I couldn't help the dirty thoughts that crossed my mind when he looked over at me. I knew I'd be thinking of him while I gave my new toys a test run.

I went back to my magazine, not wanting to stare—no matter how gorgeous my fellow straphanger was—but I could see him in my periphery and I occasionally let my eyes drift in his direction. I knew the exact moment that he noticed my bag, and I could tell from the smirk that appeared on his face that he knew exactly what was inside, or at least what *sorts* of things were inside. I expected him to say something, but he kept quiet and dug in his pocket for his phone instead. *Oh, well*, I thought, *it's not like it would lead to anything, anyway.* So I went back to reading my magazine and watching the gorgeous stranger talk on his phone…or at least listen, since he didn't seem to do much talking. Then, when the bus hit a pothole, and my bag started to tip away from me, I saw the man smile. He'd been trying to look inside my shopping bag the entire time! Part of me was embarrassed, having a stranger looking at my most private purchases, but mostly I was turned on.

Without a second thought, I closed my magazine, leaned over to the stranger and whispered, "So, like what you see?" He shoved his phone in his pocket, not bothering to hang up—there was no one on the other end, after all—and smiled. "I'm afraid I can't answer that," he told me, "because I don't know if you're asking if I like you or your new toys."

I smiled at his relaxed response and clarified. "Both," I said.

"Well, in that case, yes."

We were nearing my stop, the bus only a few blocks away from it now, and I briefly wondered what to do about my new friend. I knew what I *should* do—ignore him and get off the bus without a second thought—but I saw no reason to deprive either of us of the pleasure I knew we could bring each other. "I'm planning to give them a spin when I get home. Care to be my guinea pig?" He didn't say anything, but when I stood a moment later and moved to the doors, he followed. And he continued following me as we left the bus and went to my apartment.

The minute we were inside the apartment he had me up against the wall, his hands pulling my skirt up to get to my ass and his tongue pushing between my lips. His knee came up between my legs, pressing against my pussy, and it was then that I realized how wet I was, how ready. I moaned deeply against his mouth and then pushed him away. "Uh-uh," I said, my voice husky. "I believe we have some more pressing matters to deal with first." With that, I dragged him into the bedroom and dumped the bag of toys onto the bed. His eyes went wide when he saw all the things I'd bought. There was the slim, plastic G-spot vibrator to replace my old one, of course, but there was also a pair of vibrating nipple clamps; a small, red leather paddle; a clear, sparkly butt plug; a strange C-shaped vibrator that the salesgirl told me could be worn during sex and a new strap-on kit. After I'd spread everything out atop the comforter, I looked back at the stranger. His eyes were wide with surprise, but there was something else there, too—lust. He wanted to use my toys as much as I did, and I was more than willing to share.

He looked over at me and smiled, and that was it. I quickly became the aggressor, lunging at him and shoving him against my dresser while I attacked his mouth, my tongue begging entrance while our lips slid sensuously against each other. As soon as he let me in, I moved to the next step and started to tug at his shirt, untucking it from his jeans and hurriedly pulling at the buttons to get it off him. He didn't need me to tell him that he should start undressing me, too, and as I worked the stubborn buttons with my trembling fingers, he unzipped my skirt and forced it down my legs, my panties going with it. I gave up on his shirt buttons then, realizing he had me half-naked and I had yet to get even one article of clothing off of him. Pulling back, I tugged his button-down and undershirt over his head and threw them on the floor next to us. His pants were next, and when they pooled at his ankles, he kicked off his flip-flops and stepped out of the pile of denim. If I'm being honest, he wasn't the most gorgeous naked man I'd ever seen, but he was the most attractive man in my apartment at the moment, and a most willing participant in my sex games, so his being naked, finally, only enhanced his appeal.

Dropping to my knees, I took his half-hard cock into my mouth and started sucking, not to get him warmed up—there were more than enough toys to tempt him with—but because I wanted to more than I'd ever wanted to suck cock before. I spent only a few minutes on my knees, though; there was so much more I wanted to do with him.

He reached for the nipple clamps as I stood up, but I took them from him and shook my head. As much as I loved to have my nipples played with, I wanted to test out the dainty rubber-coated clamps on him, instead. He looked surprised as I reached over and tweaked his right nipple, pulling it with my fingers, extending it just far enough so that the clamp would have something to grab on to. Then I did the same thing to the left one and when both clamps were screwed tightly into place, I pulled the tabs from the battery compartments and pressed the buttons to turn them on. As the first vibrations shot though his nipples, he threw his head back and moaned; he liked it! I smiled and dropped a hand to my throbbing pussy; the sight of him enjoying himself so much was almost unbearably arousing.

This time, *he* stopped *me*. "Oh, no," he said, "not when there are so many better options." He quickly picked up the vibrator and turned it on, pressing it against my mound. I had to admit, it was better than having to do all the work myself, and having someone else—a hot, sexy male someone else—controlling the teal-colored toy only enhanced the sensations.

I could feel my pussy start to throb even more, aching to have the plastic phallus deep inside. He teased me for a while longer, though, tracing my lips with the toy, then leaving my mound altogether and running the vibrator over my inner thighs, my stomach, my ass. Every touch of the vibrator set me on fire and made me want him more. When he finally, unexpectedly, shoved the vibrator into my pussy, at last making contact with my G-spot, I came explosively. The buildup had been too much to take, and when the smooth plastic eased between my lips with the help of my copious juices, it was all I could do not to just end things there. As it was, I had to grab on to his shoulders to keep myself from melting into a puddle at his feet. I had no idea what was turning me on more, the vibrator or the man wielding it, but it didn't matter; I wasn't about to give up either of them.

With the nipple clamps still buzzing away on his chest, making his shoulders and abs ripple each time a shiver of excitement shot through him, he pulled my vibrator from my pussy and picked up the next toy: the butt plug. I wasn't sure who he would use it on, me or himself, and when he pushed it between my pussy lips, I was even more confused. Did he not know what it was? "This is a—" I started to explain, but he cut me off with the most sensual kiss I'd ever had. "I know what it is," he said when he pulled his mouth from mine. He demonstrated his knowledge a moment later when he removed the plug from my pussy and pushed the tip against my puckered asshole. "It needed a little lube," he said by way of explanation, and I just nodded my head, too excited to speak. He started to push the butt plug inside me then, and I felt my sphincter open up for the narrow finger-sized head before closing around the narrower joint. My ass opened wider still for the lower half of the sparkly plug, which was as thick as two fingers at its widest point, and then gripped the narrow point right above the flared base. He held the plug in place for a moment, making sure my ass wouldn't release it, and then pulled his hand away, leaving the rubber toy held securely between my cheeks.

I leaned up to kiss him then, and when the nipple clamps vibrated against my chest, I felt my ass clench tightly around the butt plug in ecstasy. My pussy was starting to throb again, and I knew I needed to be filled—preferably by my playmate's dick—before I went crazy. It seemed that my sexy stranger had similar desires, because when he pulled me closer, I felt his cockhead brush my stomach. We stood like that a moment, his hardness teasing me, touching me everywhere except where I wanted it. Then he grabbed the little purple C-vibe, threw me back onto the bed and shoved it into me, turning it on as he did so. I could feel it vibrating against my clit and my G-spot, not too strong, but enough to keep me on edge, and then I felt his cock sliding into me, too. He wasn't huge, but he filled me nicely, and his cock forced the inner arm of the vibrator to press more firmly against my G-spot. Let me just say that, oh, my god, it was amazing! I'd never been so full from a vibrator, and no cock had ever sent such a continuous wave of pleasure through me; the combination of the two was intense. I couldn't imagine ever having sex without that little purple toy ever again. And then he started thrusting into me from above.

Everything I'd felt before was suddenly magnified a thousand times. As he pulled out, the vibrations weakened and my pussy felt unbearably empty, but every inward thrust brought deep vibrations, deeper than any vibrator had gone before, and a feeling of fullness that I couldn't imagine getting with anyone else. My ass clenched the plug inside of it with each stroke of his cock, the double penetration delighting me, and the dual vibrations, wow! After a half-dozen thrusts, I was coming again, unable to control my climax, but he didn't stop. He kept pumping into me, his strokes getting faster and faster, then slowing down, and then speeding up again. He tried to keep pace with my continuous orgasms, slowing down each time a new lightning bolt of excitement shot through me and speeding up when I started to calm down. It felt like a series of waves crashing inside my pussy, and I didn't know how much longer I could stand it; it was almost *too much* pleasure.

Finally, he was ready to come, and through the vibrations I could feel his pounding cock start to pulse inside me. His thrusts

grew shallow as he pressed his body against mine, and I felt the
nipple clamps still vibrating against his chest—and mine, too. I
grabbed his ass, pulling his dick deeper inside me, and then moved
my hands to his chest. I plucked the clamps from his nipples and
felt him shoot into my cunt with a loud groan, the first sound
he'd made in what seemed like ages. The nipple clamps buzzed
on the bed next to us as he filled me, the vibrator between us
keeping us both on edge even through our climaxes.

Sated, he pulled out of me, taking the vibrator with him, and
collapsed next to me while all of the vibrating toys buzzed on
my other side, draining their batteries as they'd drained ours.
The butt plug rested forgotten in my ass for a few more minutes.
When he gently pulled it out for me, I had one last climax, my
body so weak from the seemingly dozens of others I'd had earlier
that I could barely react to the pleasure that shot through me.

Completely exhausted, I took a deep breath and closed my
eyes, my body going limp against the mattress. For a split second
I wondered if we'd get around to testing out the strap-on, but I
didn't think it was the right time to ask. We needed to rest before
we did anything else.

I was awakened almost as soon as I dozed off, the bed jostling
me violently. When I opened my eyes, I realized that I was still
on the bus. We'd just hit a pothole, and when I looked over to
check my bag, I saw it tilted toward the sexy stranger two seats
over. He had his phone to his ear, as though he were listening to
someone talking on the other end, but his eyes were glued to my
bag as he tried to get a peek at my purchases, which had shifted
around enough to offer him the briefest glimpse.

"Like what you see?" I asked boldly, catching his eye. He
smirked. "I need someone to help me test them out. You interested?" I asked. He didn't say anything, but he shoved his phone
into his pocket without hanging up, confirming my suspicions

that there was no one on the other end, and stood when I did. He followed me off the bus at the next stop and down the street to my apartment. As I unlocked the door, I made a note to break out the strap-on sooner, not wanting it to be left out this time around.

LET'S DANCE

D. L. King

Hands up in the air, twirling around trancelike, eyes closed, with a stupid smile on his face—or maybe it was more a beatific smile. Actually, I've seen that same look before, seen it a lot. I mean the whole thing, like if he had been tied that way and suspended, his body set to twirling in the air. But this wasn't like that. This was on a dance floor at a club. A regular, vanilla club. I'm just saying...

Patty had convinced me to go out for drinks after a particularly long day—week—year at work, and we'd ended up in this cool-kid college bar. Not our usual kind of place, but it had a happy hour. We'd been scoping out the field, discussing each guy's assets—and ass—in great detail. "Hey, Eve, what about that loon?" she asked me.

I followed her finger and saw him. She was laughing but I was thinking, *Oh, how sweet.*

"What?" She looked at me like I was insane. "What?" I said again. "He's adorable. Just look at him." A laugh and the scent of gin wafted toward me. "C'mon. You don't think he's cute?" More laughter. "Seriously. He's just into the music. I think it's sweet."

"Somebody needs another drink," she said as she pulled me back toward the bar.

I didn't really want another drink, but I played along. With two fresh martinis, one vodka and one "real," we wandered back to our previous lookout. Cute Boy was still on the dance floor, this time dancing with another guy and girl. The three of them looked like they didn't have a care in the world.

When the music changed, his friends left the floor and I decided to go for it. Handing my drink to Patty, I danced my way into the crowd. From behind, I put my hands on his hips and he jumped. He tried to turn to see what was going on but I pressed my body to his back, grabbing his prominent pelvic bones and grinding myself against his ass.

I could feel his pulse speed. He was a gazelle. I was stronger and more powerful. And I was hungry.

"Um, Alice?"

"Who's Alice?" I asked.

"Oh. I thought maybe you were Al...coming back from the bar. Do I know you? I mean, it's all right. I mean, who...?"

"No, you don't know me." I moved my hands in from his hips, and down, keeping the pressure on. "Would you like to?"

"Uh-huh." He put his hands over mine and we continued to dance, my fingers stroking his cock through his jeans.

I love those baggy pants, especially on skinny white boys. You can hide an embarrassment of riches in there. My hands just naturally found their way past the waistband to his naked cock. That was when his hands grabbed mine from the outside.

"Aren't you just the cutest thing? Did somebody shave you? And, by the way, do something else with those hands, unless you want me to go away." He let my hands go and tentatively reached back to cup my ass.

"Like what you feel?" I asked as my fingers found damp balls and toyed with them. As I worked my way slowly back toward his hole he almost collapsed forward.

"I was right: you are adorable," I said. Moving my hands back, I gently squeezed his balls. "Have a girlfriend?" He shook his head. "Have a boyfriend?" He laughed. "Keeper?" He shook his head again and turned back to see who was tormenting him. "What's your name?"

"Pete."

"Wanna go somewhere, Pete?"

"I…"

"Yes?" I asked. I pinched the tip of his cock and squeezed his balls with my other hand. He jumped. "Oops," I said.

"I…"

He jumped again when I pulled my hands from his pants, slammed them onto his hips and moved him away from my body. "Oh, well."

"No, wait. Yes. I mean, yes."

"Good answer." Keeping my hands on his hips, I led him off the dance floor, toward Patty and my drink. I put my arm around his waist and picked up my martini. "Patty, this is Cute Boy. Cute Boy, this is Patty," I said as I took a healthy swig of vodka.

"Pete," he said, reaching out his hand to Patty.

As Patty reached for Pete's hand, I put my empty glass in hers. "I gotta take Cute Boy home now. See you next week." I could hear her bark of laughter as I guided Pete to the door.

Once on the street, Pete put his arm across my shoulder. "What's your name?"

"Eve. Short for Evangeline. But I haven't decided whether you get to use it or not." I hailed a cab.

He looked so bewildered. He wasn't at all drunk. "What do you mean I don't get to use it? What am I supposed to call you?"

Once in the cab, I said, "Hey, Cute Boy, who shaved your boy parts?"

A blush began at the top of his ears and traveled to his cheeks. "Um, I did," he said.

"What made you decide to do something like that?" The blush spread to his forehead and neck simultaneously, and he looked at the floor of the cab. "Aw, c'mon, you can tell me." I rested my hand on the inside of his thigh and gave him a good-natured squeeze. He shifted in his seat and looked at me. It looked as if he was trying to gauge my politics—or where I might stand on certain topics—or maybe whether he could trust me. Whatever he was thinking, the body butt I gave his shoulder must have swayed him.

"Well, see, I was reading this book...and the guy in it—I guess it was a dirty book..." He looked out the window at the Manhattan Bridge. "Where do you live?"

"Brooklyn. Go on."

"So, yeah, anyway, this guy was in this experiment and the women who were doing the experiment had to shave him, see." I nodded my head. "And he seemed to like it. The way it felt. In the book. And I thought maybe I might like it too."

"And do you?" The blush got more prominent as did the tent in his jeans. "Cute Boy, you're so cute."

"I'm kinda embarrassed. I just did it last night. Didn't know if I could, well, be with anyone—this way, you know?" He shot a glance at the back of the cabdriver's head.

Where was HBO when you needed them? The driver wasn't paying any attention. He was on his cell, having a heated discussion, in low tones, in an unrecognizable language as the cab shot across the bridge.

"Brooklyn?"

"Don't worry about it. It's not a foreign country," I said. "I think you're gonna like it; the shave, I mean. Anyway, you'll know pretty soon, one way or another. And I've decided: you can call me Miss."

The cab stopped. I paid the driver and waited for Pete to get out.

"You live *here*?" he asked. He gazed up at the six-story Red Hook building that had done duty as a warehouse at the turn of the century and was now artists' lofts.

"Yeah," I said. "And we have the whole place to ourselves." The elevator opened onto a large, open, industrial space. Photographic equipment was off to one side; a couch and two overstuffed chairs faced away from the windows, toward a big flatscreen TV, leaving the window side of the room empty.

"Make yourself comfortable. My roommate's out of town, on a photo shoot. He does fashion and fetish. What would you like to drink?" I asked from the kitchen.

"I was drinking beer at the bar. Eve, right? This is awesome."

I handed him a bottle of Beck's. "That's 'Miss' to you. Take off your clothes. I want to see if you did a good job." He looked at me, and then at the windows, which looked out onto the harbor and darkness. "It's okay, Cute Boy; no one's gonna see you except me." I slid his T-shirt up over his abs and past his chest. I loved the little patch of black hair he had between his pecs and around his nipples. I ran my hands over them and he sighed. The scent of beer lingered. "Come on, Cute Boy, chop, chop. Let's go." I raised the shirt higher and he pulled it over his head.

"You were adorable, dancing at the bar. I loved the way you had your hands in the air, sort of like you were in another world." I unbuttoned his pants. Oversized, they immediately slid down to his ankles, leaving him completely naked. Pete's hard-on curved to the right. "Don't you think it makes your cock look bigger?"

"What?" he said, reaching for the buttons on my blouse.

"Later, maybe, if you're very good," I said. I brushed his hands away and ran mine up his shaft. "Shaving off your pubic hair," I said. "It makes your cock look bigger." He shuddered and tried to bump himself against me. "Doesn't it feel nice in the air, bare like that? I bet you've hardly been able to keep your mind on anything else, or your hands off, ever since you did it." I ran my hand softly over the shaved skin around the root of his cock. "Isn't that right?" I could see precome beginning to leak from the tip.

He groaned. "Don't you wanna get naked?" he asked.

"Ever been tied up?" He watched my mouth as if I were speaking a foreign language. "I know what kind of book you were reading."

My hands explored his hot skin and I felt the familiar cunt tingle I always get at the start of the game. Naked boys, especially when I'm clothed, just do it for me. My breath hitched as I reached for his balls and gently rolled them around in my palms.

He shook his head no.

"Wanna be?"

His cock waved. "Um..."

"Yeah, I guess you do, don't you?" I looked him in the eye and nodded. He copied the nod as he looked at me. "I do the rigging for my roommate on some of his shoots." He just stared at me as I fondled him. "I tie his models up."

"Oh," he said. "Oh. Okay." Goose bumps appeared on his chest and arms.

"All right, so, if you don't like it, or you want to stop, you have to say, *I'm done*, understand? If you say anything else, I might not know what you mean, so you have to say, *I'm done*."

"I got it," he said. "It's just like in the book I was reading. Oh, my god."

I spread a blanket on the floor by the window and had him stand in the center. I began with a utilitarian chest harness. The pattern incorporated diamonds in both back and front as well as two horizontal ropes falling above and below his nipples. Checking in with him, I asked him how he was doing.

"Fine," he said. "This is fun."

I ran my hands over his imprisoned nipples and watched the waves of goose bumps travel up and down his chest. "Nice, huh? Everything feels more intense in the ropes, doesn't it?" His body gave a little involuntary shake, and I set to work on his thighs and groin.

Putting double wraps around each thigh at three separate points, I joined them on both the outside and inside of his legs. I brought the tails from his back tie down the crack of his ass and up between his legs. Pulling them tight, I tied them off at the waist.

"How does that feel," I asked, running my fingers up and down the rope that stretched his asscheeks apart.

"Fuck," he said. "That's so amazing."

I ran my hands between his legs on either side of his straining cock and gave the taut, smooth skin just above his erect shaft a smack.

"Oh, my god, don't stop," he said.

"We're not done yet. Plenty of time to play later. More work to be done yet. Keep your pants on, so to speak. Raise your arms with your hands in the air, like when you were dancing."

I wrapped each arm separately and brought the tails down

his back and between his legs, wrapping and separating his balls, before creating a rope cock ring. "Still good?" I asked.

"Yeah, but if I lower my arms, all the tension's gone."

"Don't worry, just be patient." I helped him lie down on the blanket and then lifted his arms over his head again, spreading them wide and fastening his wrists to a stretcher bar. By the time I finished with the stretcher bar, he was drifting off into sub space. It seems Cute Boy was a total bondage slut. The noise of the electric winch snapped him out of his trance.

"What's going on?"

"I'm going to suspend you. I think you'll like it." I attached the ropes from the pulley system to three strategic points on his back and waist harness, making sure his weight was evenly distributed, then I attached the spreader bar to the pulley system as well. I supported him as the winch began to lift him from the floor. When he was vertical again, I wrapped his calves to his ankles and lifted first one leg, then the other, off the ground, bending his knees and fastening his ankles about a foot from his thighs so it looked like he was jumping.

"Okay?" I asked.

"Amazing," he replied. "Please say you have a camera. You gotta have a camera!"

I laughed and held him by the balls, rocking him back and forth, looking into his eyes. "You're a lot of fun, Cute Boy." As I ran my hands over his shaved groin and my fingers along the sides of the rope separating his ass, he began to shake in his harness. I played with the precome at the tip of his cock and stroked the underside.

"You want to come?"

"Oh, yeah," he moaned.

"What's my name?"

"Eve."

I smacked his ass.

"Miss, Miss!" he yelled.

"I like this smooth skin, Cute Boy," I said, stroking the newly shaved skin. A combination of touch and gentle humiliation brought him off and, once he was done, I lowered him back to earth and removed the ropes.

After some cookies and cuddling, we exchanged numbers and as I walked him to the door he glanced over at my desk. "Hey, that's the book," he said.

I looked down. "That book?"

"Yeah, that's the book I was reading."

"No shit? I wrote that book," I said, handing him the sequel.

THAT GIRL

Cherry Bomb

I am a promiscuous girl...

...only not in the way that you think. Oh, I know what they say about me. I hear them back home, clamoring in judgment, their whispers. They don't even wait until my back is turned anymore. I know what they think of me, which is why the second that you show any interest in me, any desire to get to know me, they will come to you with the same words on their lips:

"Watch out for that one. She's dangerous."

And I guess I am. What else would you call someone like me? Someone so emotionally reckless, a dangerous fuck. I am the girl that wants everyone and everything, the girl with the uncontrollable lust and insatiable hunger.

But color me misunderstood. It's never just the sex that I want. Fucking just for fucking's sake is devoid of my trademark longing and romance. It's base, animalistic, and I am nothing if not emotionally evolved. Sex is an exchange. Sex is what I use to tap people like maple trees, driving through their bark, and waiting for that delicious, liquid inner core to come slowly dripping out into my hands, into my heart. It isn't done casually, ever, because I am one half of that attachment, that tangle of hands and lips and hearts and tongues. I am excruciatingly devoted; if you let me in, my heart will never let you go, and all I want is everything.

I have tried, in the past, to indulge in the anonymous safety of one-night stands. There was that icy-eyed Canadian drag king, touring through town for one night. I took him home and we fucked on my little bed, both of us sheepish and messy in the morning. But that wasn't good-bye, and a few weeks later I was flown up to Canada to whisper, "Please fuck me," into his ear and spend a weekend in bed. But his sweet nature drew me in, and we are still friends. There was a birthday present in L.A. and another some years later, all failed attempts to create an air of casualness around my fucking. But my ruling planet Venus reared her head and reminded me how deeply my body remembers. It always goes straight to my heart.

Love is my communion and sex the sacred, blessed wafer. "This is the body, given to you," offered to outstretched tongues and eyes cast upward. Longing for redemption. Fucking is as close to redemption as I will ever be.

And I know why they think what they do, my messy lust overflowing and disturbing all of those boundaries they like so much. And I can't, or I won't, control myself, despite the guilt I feel at always wanting so much...always needing so much from the people who seem to want to give it. I know I shouldn't, but I do anyway.

I fucked my cousin because I couldn't stand not running my fingers over those lines next to her mouth, or the way her eyes watched me from across the table. My feverish little mind loved fucking my cousin, even if she isn't really my cousin.

I let my mind and my eyes wander slowly over the face of my former Brooklyn drag king, my lids raised just enough to let him know that I am thinking about that weekend we spent in a hotel room on the beach. We fucked and I drove. He remembers.

I fantasize about my best friend's roommate, the one roped *off-limits* with yellow caution tape, only making me want her more. I dream up clandestine Sunday morning fucks, her hand over my mouth to try and keep me quiet, keep me secret, while she works her fingers in and out of slickness that she is responsible for. I imagine the exquisite pain inflicted from my precise leather straps, and in my head I know that is what we both need.

I ache for philosophy professors with Italian accents, strong arms pushing me up against the backs of cars and lips meeting for the first time. I daydream about those fingers dragging slow circles across my hip bones, teasing and conflicted, while I grab the back of her neck and whisper in her ear, "I just want to be close to you."

My head is completely filled with thoughts of that tattooed blonde lawyer, her hands tracing paths she's already worked out in her mind. My heart is pumping the fear of love hard into my chest and she slides her fingers inside me and says, "Tell me how wet you are. Tell me how much you want me to fuck you."

Sex is my resolution, my bond, my promise for retribution. I dream of wielding sex like Lady Vengeance, enticing my former musician love away from her meek new girlfriend, coaxing her into my bed and winning her back between my sheets. That's the way it always was for the two of us...love folded over anger, the former triumphing over the latter, rising like a phoenix. We were the story of fucking as survival...

Or the one who just slammed the door and walked out after scribbling, *I love you no matter what,* onto a birthday card. She got all of me, body and heart, that first time we fucked on her bed in front of an open window.

I just want someone to see me. More than being looked at, I want to be seen. And there is no greater moment of clarity for me than being hot and spent, tangled between sheets, skin on skin...

OZ

Isabelle Gray

*H*ome

I want you to fuck me like you've been in prison for seven years for doing very bad things. I want your hair to be long and greasy from a lack of access to the proper grooming products. I want you to smell clean but industrial. I want you a little nervous because you never know who might shiv you from behind. I want to feel an uncomfortable chill curling around my spine when you look at me because you've forgotten what it's like to be near a woman. I want your body covered in ominous, fading ink. I do not want you to kiss me gently. I want you to kiss me like you're going to eat my face, like you're going to chew my lips, swallow them whole. I want you to hold me so tight my ribs crack. I don't want you to let me breathe. I want you to make loud ugly sounds that frighten and repulse me. I want you to throw me against a wall so hard we hear the drywall crack. I want you to use coarse language. Don't you dare say sweet things. Call me dirty. Call me a whore. Make it all true. You'll have to have some stubble on your face, just enough to make me raw. I want you to be greedy. Don't tear my clothes off. That would be a cliché. Instead, pull my T-shirt over my head like I'm a little girl. Fold it neatly. Set it on the floor. Unbutton my jeans, shimmy them down my legs. Take hold of each knee, lifting my feet free, then pull the jeans away. Fold those, too. Set them on top of my T-shirt. I'm not wearing any underwear. Let's not pretend. Grab my breasts. Let them spill between your fingers. When we finally end up on the floor, I want you to roll me onto my stomach so I'm wondering if old habits are hard to break, so I'm wondering if this is how you and your cellmate got down after lights out. Sweat all over me. Sweat so much I feel you curving along my waist and under me. Plant a hand at the base of my neck. Tighten your grip. Fill me with your cock. Fuck me hard. Split me in two, then put me back together. Tell me how to move. Slap that ass. Tell me what to say back to you. When you're done, just before you fall asleep, your body sticky and heavy on mine, say thank you because there is no place like home.

Wicked

I want you to kneel. I want your forehead pressed to the floor, your wrists crossed one over the other against the small of your back. I want you to tremble. I need you to fear. When I bring the flat of my hand to the curves of your ass, I want you to breathe deeply. In. Out. I want you to whimper, then still. Anticipate. Wait a little more. When your skin starts to cool, and the red from my hand begins to fade, I want you to want. Wait. And then I want you to ask. When I don't respond, I want you to beg. Beg until your voice is hoarse, until the only thing that will sustain you from one moment to the next is my hand on your ass harder and harder until the pain evolves into pleasure and then becomes something else entirely. I want to see your cock hard. I want to see it throb, with a thin stream of silver oozing from the tip. When my hand grows weary, I want you to stand and when I look in your eyes, I want to see surprise as I drop to my knees. I'm going to kiss your thighs, feel the muscles strain beneath my lips. I'm going to wrap my fingers around the base of your cock, squeeze. Let my breath fall on you. Wait. When I wrap my lips around you, I want you to cry. I'm going to dig my fingernails into your tender ass and smile around your cock as you hiss. I'm going to swirl my tongue around the tip, and it's going to grow more swollen and red. Your legs will tremble more. You'll barely be able to stand up. You'll whisper, *"Please."* I will show you mercy. I will swallow you whole. Slowly, slowly, I'll work my mouth along the length of you. I'll allow you to grip my head with your calloused hands. I'll relax my throat and my eyes will tear as you fuck my mouth. My chest will tighten as I struggle to breathe. I will twist your balls, hard. You'll gasp, groan. When you can't control yourself anymore and you're making sounds that frighten us both, I want you to come in my mouth. After you slump to the floor, trying to catch your breath, I want you to say, "You are a wicked, wicked witch."

Yellow Brick Road

Run me a bath. The water should be hot, so hot the bathroom fills with steam and we're forced to leave the door open to find a breath of fresh, cool air. The water should smell sweet, the better for you to eat me with. When I lower myself into the tub, I want it to feel so good I sigh. Bring a radio, set it on counter. Find something good, something older, maybe James Taylor. Kneel at the side of the tub. Roll up your sleeves, hum under your breath. I love the way you hum. Squeeze some soap into a large, soft sponge. Start with my arms; scrub my body in firm, slow circles. Take your time where it matters. There. And there. There, too. Wash me clean. I have a birthmark, a long narrow line that runs from the base of my neck, between my breasts, over my stomach, right down to my cunt like a thin scar holding me together. Take your clothes off. Join me in the tub. Say something funny. I want to laugh. Kiss me softly, so softly I can barely feel your lips against mine, so softly I want nothing more than every inch of your body pressing against mine. Kiss my chin. Kiss my neck. Trace the column of my throat with your tongue and suck the skin of my neck between your teeth. Make my back arch. Leave a necklace of bruises around my throat. It's cold outside. I want to wear a turtleneck. Roll my nipples between your thumbs and forefingers, but don't be gentle about it. I want to feel this tomorrow. Give me that sharp, almost painful twinge of pleasure at the base of my spine. Say something dirty when I cup my hand between my thighs, when I touch my clit, when I stroke, when I moan softly. Lift me out of the tub and carry me, dripping wet in more than one way, to our bed. I won't mind that we get the sheets wet. Draw your lips, your tongue, along my birthmark. Kiss my pussy mound, shaved bare just for you. Spread my lips with your fingers. Lick me. Lick me. Taste inside me. Follow the yellow brick road.

Over the Rainbow

On a hot day, after it's rained and the sky is a hazy orange, surprise me. Call and tell me to meet you in one of the homes you're building. When I pull up, wait for me on the driveway, surrounded by dirt, a Dumpster, plywood, plaster. Wear dirty jeans, covered in paint stains, a flannel shirt over a wife-beater, steel-toed boots. Before we go inside, point up to the sky and the colorful glow arcing above us as the water all dries. Hold my hand, tell me to be careful as I step over a hole in the floor, avoid stray nails. Take me to a blanket you've laid on the newly installed hardwood floors. Undress me slowly, letting your fingers linger as my clothes fall away. Lie down with me, you on your side, me on my back. Tell me you've been thinking about me all day. Tell me how you've been thinking about me all day. Be explicit.

Trace around my nipple with your tongue, but don't reach for it, not yet. Watch me shiver as your breath falls on my skin. Slide your hand, fingers splayed along my birthmark, and don't wait. Fill me with two of your fingers. As you thrust in and out, twist your wrist. Fuck me faster. Drape one of your legs over mine. I'll clasp the back of your neck, run my fingers through your hair, curl them into a fist of your hair. Wrap your mouth around my nipple. Squeeze it with your lips. Groan into my body. Start sucking, hard. Pull your fingers away from me so that I feel empty and hollow. Rub my wetness into my lips, pry them open, fill my mouth. Listen as I swallow your fingers and then stop teasing me. Lie on top of me, your body heavy and hairy on mine, our noses full of sawdust and paint fumes, the smell of rain. Enter me gently, fuck me rough. Show me what it's like somewhere over the rainbow.

Heart

You never say you love me. You say *ditto*. You kiss me on my forehead. You stare at me with a *look* in your eyes. I know what you feel for me. You love me straight through to your marrow and bone. And yet... When we're making love, and my hands are trying to understand your shoulder muscles, my head is thrown back and I'm spread open and wet and all of me is yours, I want you to whisper, *I love you*. I want you to say it. I want you to show me you have a heart.

MARRIED LIFE

Charlotte Stein

'm so horny I could fuck anything. That guy with the weird hair and the nervous hands—I could fuck him. I could fuck his peach-haired girlfriend, too. And is that his mother with them?

Throw her in while you're at it.

It's not my fault, however. You'd want to have sex with strangers, too, if you were prickling all over like me and your husband never wanted to do you. They say girls don't really want it like guys do—in sitcoms it's always the wife with the headache, or the wife grousing about her "duties" or the wife being some awful harpy that I'm sure wives rarely are.

But they're all wrong, because I'm a girl, and a wife, and I do want it. I want it so much that I'm melting. I melt into the floor of the train and dissolve through the metal and plastic and find my way through the tracks to the ground, to the soil, to the water in the soil and then far away, to somewhere else where I give and get pleasure.

Where I *am* pleasure, and nothing more.

* * *

I think it's mainly because of all the fantasies I used to have
before we were married and into the missionary position. My
husband is oddly handsome and as big as a tree, and I'd spend
hours imagining what it would be like to climb him.

Back when he wasn't quite mine, we used to all sit together,
this big fun group of friends, talking and laughing while I
squirmed on my chair and thought about poking my tongue into
his ear, scaling him like a city wall, catching him in the magnificent nude.

He's not muscular, exactly, but he's so *heavy* looking, as
though he could weigh you down just by removing his shirt. He
makes a person want to be consumed by him, pressed on by his
great hairy body. There's so much of him to hold on to—why
doesn't he want me to hold on?

Instead we have sex once a month, and it's awkward and
silent and barely moving, as though if he jostles me too hard I'll
collapse. I want to collapse. I'm already collapsing, with lust.

He's such a bear, that's the thing. I thought he'd be like one.
I mean, he can really snarl at assholes who rub him the wrong
way. It's not like he's soft or simpering. And those few times we
had sex before we got married were good. They were nice.

They just weren't my fantasies, and they never became them.
I thought marriage was about sharing all those things you were
afraid to before, but he seems even more afraid and I never got
off the starting blocks. I never said: *I want us to tie each other
up, I want to fuck in fun places, I want to have sex every day
and so hard and furious that it rocks me.*

But he just doesn't seem to need anything.

So I'm left remembering when I thought things would be
amazing, mired in that teetering-on-the-brink place of long,
open-mouthed kisses, his big hands covering my tits and the idea

of him being daring enough to play. I ache thinking of those caresses now.

I ache just looking at him, sitting across the table from me. He's engrossed in the newspaper, almost ready to go to work. I could just lean over and undo that tie, slide his jacket off his big bear shoulders, get down on my knees and swallow his cock to the root until he shows me he has needs.

He must have needs, right?

He kisses me on the forehead before he heads off to work. That tiny nothing will have to last me the rest of the day.

It isn't that we're not happy. We are. We have everything in common and he's not closed off in any other area. We talk. We flirt and banter as though we've just started dating and I want to kill him—I want to *kill him* with my *sex*. All the chitter chatter is a constant prelude, conversational foreplay that never gets to the actual play.

I have to wonder if he's gay.

I mean, he likes show tunes. And when he sings I want to have sex with the sounds coming out of him. He's also very tidy and a snappy dresser, and all of his tidiness needs to be messed up along with those expensive suits I often ball up in my fists.

Once, I masturbated in a mound of his clothes. I used the handle of his hairbrush—because of course he has one. His hair is thick and luxurious and almost like a lion's mane, though darker; it's a warm, rough color, like rabbit fur.

I'd make a coat out of his hair, if I could. I'd rub a strip of it wet between my thighs.

I'm wet now, wandering around the apartment in my pajamas, pretending I don't want to do myself. There's that new filthy book that I won't need and several entertaining little toys I could use that he doesn't know I have.

I've always imagined the conversation we would get into upon his discovery of my little plastic menagerie, but it only descends into hot punishing sex—rather than what it would really descend into: his probable amusement.

He finds things funny. We have a funny life together. It's even funnier when I pick the lock on his filing cabinet in order to uncover his secret homosexuality, and find instead all the secret dirty things he's been reading.

There are pages of the stuff! Piles of it! Great jumbles of scrawled-on scraps and typed chunks and words, words, words that he likes.

Words that it takes me ten minutes to realize he *writes*.

I stop for a million years, twists of paper clutched in my hands. I need the million years just to take the first idea in—that he's been secretly reading weird loose pages of porn. The second idea—that he might actually be writing this stuff—cannot be processed.

But there are handwritten notes in the margins, in Bobby's scrawl. Things like *move this here* and *swap with page twelve*. Why would he want to swap this and move that on somebody else's work? He's an accountant. He accounts things. He does not edit erotica.

He just writes it, apparently, instead.

Of course, at first I don't dare read it. I see words like *cock* and *clit* and decide it's better for my sanity that I don't. What if it's *hotter* than I've been imagining? What if it's so hot that I can't take it?

He must be jerking off if he's writing stuff like this. Doesn't it turn him on to do it? It turns me on just thinking about it.

I rifle through the pages at first, skimming, then progressing to something that isn't quite skimming. Occasionally I hide behind a cushion, though I don't think it's because the material embarrasses me. My cheeks are hot and red, but that's for an entirely different reason.

One that gets more pronounced when I read the words: *Sweat beaded on his great arched back.*

I mean, it doesn't seem like much. But despite its seeming smallness, the words trail through my mind on a permanent loop. They caress the insides of my eyelids: *his great arched back.*

I picture something slablike, honey-golden, thick and meaty: my husband's back, as he heaves a huge axe, and cleaves heavy knots of wood in two.

Of course he has never actually done anything like that in real life, but I'm sinking into the syrupiness of the image, anyway.

I fear what the rest of his words will do to me. I've already jammed my back up against the wall below the window, crouched like something feral, face too hot to bear, pussy too hot to bear, too. It swells and presses tight against the material of my pajama bottoms, humming and waiting for me to continue.

So I do. I read the words: *As she towered over him...*

She? Towering? And there's more: *Her boots gleamed so that he was certain he might see his face in them, though he did not dare look. Looking would mean that he had raised his gaze, and that was not permitted. Not here, in their secret and most private place.*

I try to stop it, but it comes on anyway: jealousy, over the use of the word *their.* I mean, I don't think he's cheating on me. I don't think he'd ever cheat on me, though of course he could be cheating on me.

But somehow the words read like a fantasy, rather than a thing that's really happened. These are my husband's secret fantasies, and they are the farthest thing from what I could have imagined. In one of them, a naughty little minx in leather teases and torments her lover for what seems like hours.

It seems like hours reading it. First I have to slog up this hill: *He twisted his body up, reaching for her mouth with his painfully taut cock. But she would not allow it. Her crimson lips, slippery with spit and his own juices, twisted into a tormenting smile.*

And then I have to contend with this: *She knelt before him, twisting and pinching her own nipples. Each little motion seemed to run right to the core of her, making her shiver before his fevered gaze. It was almost as much a relief to him as it seemed to her, to see her slide her fingers between the pouting red lips of her streaming cunt.*

I don't get to the end of it. I see other things, many other sexy scenarios and all of them stranger and less like Bobby than the last, but I don't make it to the ends of any of them. Instead, I press one finger to my well-oiled clit, and come, and come, and come.

He seems like an alien to me when he comes home, I'll admit. I think I look at him like that, too. Like he's suddenly grown a new skin over his old skin, and this was the real him all along. I mentally catalogue all of the things he's never told me he likes: Watching girls masturbate while tied up. Being made to kiss the shoes of a well-booted dominatrix. Having his arsehole licked. Licking someone *else's* arsehole. Having his nipples pinched—sometimes with things that are not fingers.

And I know that it could be that he doesn't like these things at all. Maybe he just writes what some publisher wants, having fallen into the whole thing quite by mistake.

Though somehow I doubt it.

They felt like fantasies. They were written with a strange kind of restraint, as though the writer was almost afraid of what he was saying or thinking. If the stories had been bubbly and fun and silly, I would have known he didn't mean it.

But restraint says he does. And I'm just dying to ask: Why? Why do you feel you have to be restrained? Don't be restrained. Oh, god—don't be. Don't be restrained all over me and under me and inside me. I have to get ahold of myself when he kisses me on the cheek, because I almost grab him by his tie and swallow his mouth with my own.

The earlier orgasms have done nothing to take the edge off. My nipples are suddenly stiff beneath my T-shirt. I walk with my legs tight together, so that the seam of my jeans presses against the seam of my pussy. After a second of that, I'm almost moaning.

And then he takes off his suit jacket!

I think of the story with the businessman tied to a chair, his solid sweaty chest revealed to some nasty tease's gaze, his suit jacket spread like wings. Give me a chance, Bobby. Be daring. I won't let you down. I'll step up to the plate. I will. I hardly think I can do it, but I know I could do it for him. I need to do it and not just for him. I need sex and I don't mind how he wants it.

As long as it's me he wants to wield the whip. To crawl on the floor. To tie myself up and tie him up and Bobby, don't you understand that it doesn't matter?

I burn those words into his back with mind powers I don't have. He already has command of the cooker and is opening a jar of spaghetti sauce as he drawls away about his day. I love hearing about his day because he always puts funny and interesting spins on everything, as he cooks meals I could never. I can't even boil a pan of spaghetti.

He's a good man, my husband. I want to be good to him in return.

And I think I know how to go about it.

"You're jumping like a bean today, Cal," he says, as we scarf down the spaghetti. Or at least, *I* scarf down the spaghetti. He just watches me eat as fast as I can with his big, amused eyes.

* * *

It seems like ages before we make it to bed. After dinner, he had
wanted to watch a little TV like we usually do, and then he wanted
to take a shower, and I can see his book waiting for him on his
bedside table. It's going to be forever until he goes to sleep.

And I can't do what I plan to do until he's unconscious.

By the time he's in bed and through one chapter of his book
and leaning over me to say, "Night, Cal," I'm fizzing and popping
like I don't know what. I can feel my clit all stiff and just begging
me to touch it, but I resist. It'll be better if I do.

Even when he's finally asleep, I wait and wait and wait until
I know he's deep enough in for me to exact my plan—the belt
from my dressing gown for his wrists, which are close enough
to the headboard for me to secure them thoroughly. The little
riding crop I bought for him to one day use on me is in my hand.
It has feathers on one end of it for reasons that hardly become
clear, until I trail them over his bare back. The sight alone—red
on golden skin—is enough to make me weak with thoughts of
his stories, of all the options in between teasing and torment and
pleasure and pain that we've never explored together.

It pushes me to be quick, even as I force myself to be slow.
Only a fine soft tickle to begin with. Even if he were awake, he'd
probably struggle to feel it. But I imagine it's seeping into his
subconscious all the same.

Sure enough, when I stroke a little harder he jerks his shoulder
back as though trying to nudge away a fly. He grunts with displea-
sure, and this odd freeing laughter bubbles up inside me.

I'm such a tease. I'm so naughty.

Now I'm playing the feathers right along the curve of his
spine, pressing enough that anyone could feel it. The person in
the apartment across the street could probably feel it, if he really
wanted to.

But still he doesn't wake up. He sighs, instead, as though something very satisfying has just happened. I test the feathers out on my own arm, just to see what that very satisfying thing might be—and then wish I hadn't. I almost fall over.

Maybe after, he will run this thing all over me. Maybe.

First I've got to get through this.

When he doesn't stir after an age of tickling, I give myself permission to be bolder. I hold my breath and snap the crop end hard against the meat of his thigh. Hard enough to wake the dead, I should think, but he's still not stirring.

He only stirs when I sting its tip against the firm swell of his left buttock. Then he feels it, all right.

He jerks and twists on the bed, the shock of a swat like that barely given a chance to sink in before he finds himself unable to turn as easily as he'd like. I see him come up against the belt I've tied around his wrists, and then he looks to see what's stopping him. The whole thing makes me shiver, and not just because the idea of him restrained is exciting.

I think of how cross he'll be, on discovering what I've found out and done. Oh, yeah, I cream a little over that thought.

"What—have you—?" he starts to say, before he manages to twist himself around and look at me over one solid shoulder. His eyes are wide and one eyebrow is raised, but I force myself to stay serious and stern. *Don't waver now, Callie.*

"I've tied you up," I tell him. "I think it's for your own good. You seem to have such trouble sharing things with me that I thought it'd be for the best if I were to slap and tickle it out of you."

I don't think I've ever seen my husband look dumbstruck and outraged and amused all at the same time before. He looks embarrassed, too, but I'm going to glide right over that. I'm going to glide over everything and get right to the good stuff.

"Don't speak. If you speak I might have to whack you in a place that might leave a mark. You wouldn't want that, would you?"

He goes to open his mouth, but then his eyes slide to one side. I can almost hear him puzzling out this particular conundrum.

"You've been hiding things from me, Bobby."

Now his eyes snap back to mine. It's a strange thing, to see him so mute and unsure. It makes me want to throw my arms around him—though I know that if I do, this will all be over and I'll never figure out who he wants to be, with me.

Or at least who he wants to be in bed.

"And as punishment, I'm afraid I'm going to have to crop your bare ass until it's stripy. But don't worry. In between these stripes, I'm going to drive you mad with this little bunch of feathers, right here. Aren't I considerate?"

I don't think considerate is the word he's thinking of right now. But I don't think the word he is bandying about in his head has anything to do with aversion, either.

"Lie on your stomach," I tell him.

When he does it, a heavy swell of arousal goes through me. I think because I expected him not to. There was definitely a moment of tension there. A pause, as though he was going to refuse. But now he's on his stomach with his hands twisted above his head, so silent that I can hear every shift and shuffle he makes.

I squeeze my thighs tight together, to stem that urgent ache. I just want to slide down what I'm sure will be his stiff cock, right now.

Instead I yank his pajama bottoms down and listen to him groan when I do it. He groans louder when I whack the crop against his bare ass, louder yet when I drag the things between his cheeks, as though I'm going to do dirtier, nastier things to him.

When he whimpers in a way I've never heard before, I stroke him with the feathers.

Unfortunately, that only seems to make him whimper all the more. I've never heard him be this vocal before—not even when we're in the middle of sex. He gasps and groans and comes close to words that sound like begging sorts of things, as I slap and smack and then stroke. He strains against the belt I've surely not tied so well.

And better than all of this: he rocks against the mattress as though he just can't help himself.

When I finally say to him that he can turn over now, I'm almost afraid of what I'm about to see. I can't imagine what his expression is going to be—angry? Miserable? The groans and sighs and the humping of the mattress had seemed to suggest otherwise, but he's kept all of this from me for so long. He must have a reason.

I'm not prepared for his burning-into-me gaze, the barely suppressed smile. He seems almost giddy in a way I'm sure a submissive shouldn't be.

Not that I care.

"You took your punishment very well, slave," I say, and he squirms against his bonds. His cock swings up to kiss his belly, as hard as I've ever seen it. Better than that—the head of his cock is slippery and glossy with precome, just begging me to clean him up. I want to stick my tongue out and reward him for getting this excited, but I don't.

Instead, I rap the crop against his stiff prick. He jumps as though electrocuted but gets out the first word he's managed since I started all of this: "Again."

So I do. I rap him again and then snap one over his left nipple, too, just for good measure. He groans loudly and pumps his hips up at nothing.

"Suck me off," he says, and my pussy flutters to hear him talk like that. It's entirely the wrong sort of words for a slave, but I've never heard him ask for so much as a back rub, never mind a blow job.

I almost give in. Almost.

"I don't think you get to give me orders, Bobby. No. Instead, you can lie there and be still while I take that big fat cock of yours into my slippery pussy. And if you move too much for my liking, or come before I tell you you can, I'm going to smack this crop across your neck and leave you with a stripe you can't explain. What do you think of that?"

I don't expect him to answer. But he does, all in a gleeful rush: "I think I love you more than I did the day I married you."

"You're going to love me even more when you see what I've got planned for you tomorrow," I say, and his eyes drift closed as though tasting the most heavenly chocolate.

I give the tip of his cock one lick before I swing my leg over his body, my clit swelling and more wetness trickling from my already soaked pussy when I realize that I've never done this before. I've never fucked him like this.

It's a whole new world opening up before us. He seems to think so, too, because he moans long and loud when I rub him through my slippery folds, coating him in all of my wetness before settling him at my greedy hole.

And then I just slide down, down, down, feeling him spread me open so completely, thrilling at the thickness of his stiff cock. I still have the crop in my hand and I tickle him under his jaw until he opens his eyes, the pleasure in them echoing my own, I'm sure.

He looks as though he's desperate to get his hands free and grind my cunt down on him, but he resists what I know he could easily do. Getting free isn't part of this game. Holding off his orgasm is, however.

When I slide myself up, keeping only the very tip of him in

me, the strain shows on his face. But it gets worse when I ease myself back down again. By the time I'm rocking my hips and rutting that little bundle of nerves inside me against the heavy thickness of him, he's biting his lip. When I start rubbing my stiff bud in time to my quickening up-and-down slides, I can see the muscles in his stomach tensing.

His cheeks flush. He groans beneath the pressure.

I'm sure he's not going to make it, until I make it so suddenly it shocks me. I shout his name and go rigid, swamped by pleasure so intense I can hardly hold on to it.

He can't hold on to it, either. He bellows like a wounded animal, hands suddenly free and on my hips so that he can clutch me to him as he comes. I feel his prick swell and spurt inside me in wrenching spasms, on and on and on until I'm worried for him.

Until I'm going to have bruises where he's got hold of me.

I'm sure he's going to collapse when he's through, but he doesn't. Instead, he wraps his arms tight around me and *laughs*; he laughs into my hair, loud and long. His hand goes to the back of my head and holds me so close to him, and then he presses kisses into the side of my face, my cheek, my mouth, everywhere.

"Oh, Callie," he says. "Callie. Please say we can do that every night."

I want to laugh with him then, though, maybe I'm crying at the same time.

"Of course we can," I say. I think of my plastic menagerie. "What do you want to try out tomorrow?"

PRINCESS

Elizabeth Coldwell

The first clue I have that this isn't going to be an ordinary birthday treat is when Melanie produces the blindfold. I received an email about an hour ago telling me to meet the girls in reception at one, so I assumed we'd be going to the Greek place round the corner for lunch. That's what we usually do when someone has something to celebrate, sharing plates of meze and bottles of dry white wine and making sure to invite the office manager, who prizes punctuality above all things, so we don't earn a reprimand from her when we finally sneak back into the office. And that's what I'm expecting, not for Mel to take out a black silk sleep mask bearing the word PRINCESS in sparkly crystals and slip it over my eyes.

"Mel, what are you doing?" I ask, trying to keep from vocalizing the sudden panic that rises at the sensation of having my vision so effectively cut off.

"Relax," she says, her voice close to my ear. "We wanted to get you something really special. After all, you're only thirty once. Trust me, you're going to love it."

Ignoring my protests, she guides me out of the building's revolving door to the pavement outside. I can hear the bustle of a busy London street on a Friday lunchtime, but the mask prevents me from seeing a thing. It's more than a little disconcerting, having to put myself in the hands of Melanie, even though she's been one of my very best friends for years. Around me, the other girls are giggling; they all have the advantage of knowing what's about to happen. I'm sure it's nothing bad, but I don't like the feeling of not being in control of this situation.

An engine is running close by us; from its tone I know it's a diesel, but that's the only clue I have until Mel says, "We booked the taxi for you. It's all been paid for in advance, so don't worry about anything. Just sit back and enjoy the ride. Oh—and don't take the blindfold off, whatever you do."

She opens the door and helps me inside. I grope around until I find the seat and sit down, allowing Mel to buckle the seat belt in place. I'm desperate to ask questions, but before I can, Mel has slammed the door shut and the taxi is pulling away from the curb.

The driver takes a sharp right, heading into the maze of backstreets which run parallel to the main road. I try to keep a note of the turns—left, then right again, so we must be heading toward Liverpool Street, I think—but he seems to be doubling back on himself and I'm soon forced to give up.

"Driver, can you tell me where we're going?" I ask, but there's no answer. Either the man has turned off the communication between himself and the back of the cab or he's deliberately ignoring me. With this blindfold on, there's no way I can tell. If his silence isn't unsettling enough, what happens next almost makes me jump out of my skin.

"Happy birthday, Princess," says a voice beside me. So I'm

not alone; someone has been sitting here all the time, watching me being guided into my seat and struggling to keep track of my surroundings. Someone male.

His voice is deep, with a well-spoken Scottish accent, which suggests he's more than likely from Edinburgh. No one I work with; no one I know. Mel has blindfolded me and left me in the company of a stranger: what kind of birthday treat is this?

"Don't worry, Princess," he says. "Nothing's going to happen that you don't want. If you feel uncomfortable at any time, just say 'watermelon.'"

He leans over and gives me a kiss on the cheek. I feel a slight stubble prickling my skin, and realize that he's not wearing after-shave. No wonder I wasn't aware of his presence, disguised as it was by the hot plastic smell of the taxi's interior.

Now his lips are on mine, tongue pushing gently till I open my mouth and let it slip inside. *Whoever he is, he knows how to kiss,* I think, leaning back slightly against the padded seat. His fingers caress my neck, spanning it easily. Scottish accent, stubbled chin, big hands: the clues are mounting up, but this man remains unknown to me. I know I could rip off the blind-fold—how would Mel know, after all, unless he decided to tell her?—but that would spoil things. The strange, fluttery excite-ment I'm feeling as he continues to kiss me and his hand moves lower, to unbutton my suit jacket, is partly generated by the fact that I can't see who I'm with or what is about to be done to me.

With my eyesight denied me, my other senses are working harder to compensate, making me more keenly aware of every noise, every touch, every scent. The taxi's engine is idling; at some point during the last couple of minutes we must have left the quiet side streets and now we're standing in traffic. Back on the main street; back, I'm sure, among curious passersby. My new friend reaches for the buttons on my blouse, and I move to stop him.

"Please, not here," I murmur. "People can look in."

"So let them," he says. "Let them see what I'm doing to you." There's an almost hypnotic quality to his voice, and I'm beginning to feel curiously safe with him. I withdraw my hand so he can continue to undress me. Once the blouse is undone, all he has to do is flick open the catch that fastens my bra in front, and my breasts are bare for him to play with. As he rolls my nipple between his finger and thumb, gently teasing it, it's almost possible to forget that anyone could be watching us, peering in as they wait to cross the road or looking down from the top deck of a passing bus.

What must they feel when they see me, a blindfolded blonde in the back of a cab, tits on display, letting a man she's never met before this lunchtime bend his head to take her nipple between his lips? Disbelief? Envy? Arousal? If only they could feel the excitement I do as he continues to suck. Under my sensible knee-length skirt, the black lacy thong I'm wearing is drenched with my juices. I want to slip it off. No, I want *him* to slip it off. I want to feel his hands easing the wisp of fabric down my thighs. I want to spread my legs for him shamelessly and have the marvelous mouth, which is still tormenting my nipple, work its magic on my sex.

I can't believe how wanton I've become since I clambered into this cab. How long has it been? Ten minutes? Twenty? And how much has this cost Mel and the girls? Maybe she's charged it to the company credit card, and our CEO is paying for me to have the most outrageous sexual experience of my life. Maybe he's even paying for the man with whom I'm having it....

Dimly, I become aware that the engine is no longer running. We seem to have parked somewhere, though by now I have no idea where. Perhaps the driver has grown tired of watching the show we're putting on in the back of his taxi through his mirror, and he's stopped so he can give us his full attention. Perhaps he's watching us with his fly unzipped and his fist stroking up and down the length of his cock. Perhaps he's planning to join in. I wonder what I would do if my birthday twosome suddenly turned into a threesome? Somehow, I have the feeling the word *watermelon* wouldn't be hovering anywhere near my lips.

"Lift your skirt for me, Princess," my fellow passenger orders. I do as I'm told, wriggling against the seat, and he grasps hold of my thong and tugs it down until it's stretched tautly between my ankles. I kick it off a little awkwardly, not wanting to be any more restricted than I already am. I hear him shuffling around, but I don't have any idea what he's doing until his big hands grasp my thighs. I just have time to register the feel of thick, shaggy hair on my skin, and then his mouth settles on my pussy. His tongue makes contact with my wet flesh, licking and probing. This is bliss; this is what every girl should receive on her birthday. He's one of those men who licks pussy because he loves it, I can tell, not one of those who treats it as a bothersome chore, or a means to get his cock sucked in return. The pace and pressure of his tongue strokes vary deliciously: sometimes long, flat sweeps cover the whole length of my crease, sometimes hard little flicks center directly on my clit.

I writhe crazily, sweat making my bum squeak against the synthetic leather seat. His hands grip the insides of my thighs tighter as his tongue brings me closer and closer to the edge. I wish I could see what he looks like as he eats me so hungrily: my juices glazing his chin, his eyes darkened with lust.

My back arches; the seat belt strap cuts into the soft flesh of my breasts, but I barely notice the discomfort. All I'm focused on is the pleasure I'm being given; the gift of a sudden, wracking orgasm that has me pushing up hard against his face, trying to extract every last drop of sensation from this moment.

He holds me gently, stills me, and then I sense that he's getting to his feet. "I hope you enjoyed your present, Princess, but this is where I get out," he tells me.

"Wait…" I reach for the blindfold, but he stops my hand.

"Not till I'm gone," he tells me firmly. I hear him moving around, rearranging himself. If he's a big man, he'll have to crouch a little in the cab's interior as he straightens his mussed-up hair and wipes his face clean with a handkerchief. I'm sure he'll be the picture of respectability as he steps out into the street—whichever street that may be.

As for me, I sit for a moment or two, almost overwhelmed by what has just happened, before hurriedly buttoning myself up again. Releasing the seat belt catch, I pat the floor around me, but I can't find my thong: either my mysterious stranger has made off with it or the driver will retrieve it when he next cleans the cab and keep it as a souvenir. It's probably the least the man deserves.

Finally, I pull off the blindfold, ready to be driven back to the office. That's when I realize the taxi is sitting in the parking lot behind our building. Mel has planned this so well: the perfect stranger; the lunchtime rendezvous that is so convenient to slip away from. I thank the driver, a thickset, middle-aged man in a replica football top. He merely smirks in response, and I get out of the cab on still-shaky legs.

Mel is waiting in reception as I walk back inside. "So, how was it?" she asks. She's obviously expecting me to bombard her with questions: Who is he? How did you find him? How did you know that was exactly what I needed?

I just smile and reply, "Well, it certainly made a change from a set lunch."

As I walk back to my desk, I'm still gripping the sleep mask, still feeling like a princess. What Mel doesn't know is that before my faceless stranger left the cab, he pushed something into my jacket pocket: a scrap of paper bearing his phone number and the words, *Call me soon.* There are knowing looks and winks from the girls who were in on the setup, but all I want to do is thank them. Thank them for a gift that I somehow know will keep on giving.

CHASING DANGER

Kristina Wright

Even after five years on the Minnesota State Patrol, Erica
Jeffries's heart beat a little faster every time the radio crackled
to life. The feeling was almost like sexual arousal. She squirmed
in her seat, feeling the stiff seam of her uniform pants rub against
her delicate skin. She got turned on by the lights and sirens she
got to use on high-priority calls, the heavy weight of the utility
belt she wore, the cold steel of her firearm. She had all the accou-
trements of authority—and it made her hot as hell.

Her partner, Jack Randolph, was driving today, so she could
let her mind drift a little. She'd known Jack since she'd started
with the state patrol, and he had been a mentor of sorts in those
first couple of years. He was a few years older than her and had
regaled her with his trooper tales and they'd become friends.
Sometimes, after a few beers, she considered more than friend-
ship with Jack. But he was a little too straight-laced for her.
What drew her to law enforcement was the anticipation of risk
and Jack, while he was a hell of an officer, wasn't the least bit

risky. She needed that edge of danger in all areas of her life, but so far she only had it on the job.

"It's addictive, isn't it?"

Erica pushed away her thoughts to focus on Jack's question. "What?"

"The excitement," he said. "You do this job long enough, you feel like you've got the world by the balls."

His words hit a little too close to home. She was happy to be one of the good guys—or girls, as the case might be—but that hadn't always been the case. Erica tried to change the direction of the conversation. "It's a hell of a ride, that's for sure."

The radio crackled to life.

"Charlie one-oh-nine," Jack said, depressing the button on the mic. "Over."

The dispatcher read off the information for their call.

Jack signed off, repeating the information. "White male, driving fast and erratic in a black car, traveling west on ninety-four. He's maybe three, four miles behind us."

"What do you want to do?"

He adjusted his mirrors and checked his speed. "I'll slow down a little bit and wait for him to catch up to us."

The highway wasn't particularly busy for a Sunday evening. It was nearly the end of their shift, and Erica was hoping this would be a quick—but exciting—bust. The roar of a car's engine brought her to attention. She could see it in the side mirror, rolling up on them at a good clip.

"See if you can make out the plate number," Jack said.

The car switched lanes to pass them on the right and for a split second Erica made eye contact with the driver. All that registered was shaggy black hair and dark, empty eyes. He gave her a cocky smirk before blowing by them. It was the smile, more than anything else, which triggered her sharp intake of breath. She knew that smile, had dreamed about it.

"Ben," she whispered, unable to contain her shock.

Luckily, Jack didn't notice her reaction. He floored it, setting them on a high-speed pursuit. Cars moved to the side to allow them to pass as the black car swerved between vehicles to hold his lead.

"Son-of-a-bitch," Jack said. "We can't catch a Charger. It has more under the hood than anything we've got."

He radioed dispatch the plate number. "Ten to one it's stolen."

The dispatcher confirmed his instincts. The car had been stolen from a parking garage in Minneapolis. "Suspect has been ID'd from the security video as Benjamin Slater, thirty-one. He has four warrants out for previous auto thefts. All units are on alert."

Erica was glad someone else had identified Ben so she didn't have to admit she knew him. The Charger disappeared on the horizon, like a phantom in the night.

The radio crackled to life again, but it wasn't the dispatcher's voice they heard. "I thought you might try a little harder to catch me."

"That bastard," Jack swore. "He has a police radio. Fuck!"

It was the first time Erica had heard Jack swear. He was always so calm and in control. It made her nervous to see him rattled.

"Stupid pigs. You think you're so fucking tough—"

Erica grabbed the mic. "Hey, Slater, why don't you pull that car over?"

There was silence on the radio for a moment, then Ben responded. "Who's this?"

Erica hesitated. Did she dare give him her real name? Would he remember her? "Erica," she said.

"Erica what?"

"Just Erica."

Benjamin laughed. "Right. Erica. Officer Erica. You the redheaded babe?" Jack snorted, but Erica couldn't help but smile. "That's me."

"You're hot. I might be willing to stop for you."

She sighed in relief. He didn't remember her. Why would he? She'd hung on the fringes of his crowd in those hazy years between high school and when she finally got her act together. They had dated only briefly—if you could call long nights of drunken sex dating—and he had quickly moved on to some other starry-eyed girl who thought being with the bad boy made her cool.

Though Erica had never actually broken any laws herself, she had been privy to a lot more than she cared to remember. One night, she had found herself in a stolen Porsche on her way to New York with Ben Slater. He had fucked her on the hood of the sleek sports car in a deserted parking lot while they waited for the buyer to arrive. They'd caught a cab to a seedy motel in the city, where he fucked her again before leaving her in a tangle of rumpled sheets to go get a pack of cigarettes. He never came back. Later, she would decide that him leaving that night had been the best thing that could have happened to her. Ben Slater was a piece of her past she'd rather forget—but here he was now, larger than life.

"Well, pull over and we'll talk."

This made Jack straighten up. "The captain's going to ream you for that little move, Jeffries, but keep him talking."

"C'mon, Slater," she cajoled. "Pull over and let's figure this mess out."

Laughter crackled over the radio. "I'm not going to make it that easy for you. You're going to have to work for me, babe."

"What do you want me to do?" Erica knew the question was

a mistake the minute it left her mouth. "I mean, what do you want?"

"Oh, baby, I'll tell you what I want you to do. I want your hot, wet mouth wrapped around my dick—"

"That's enough," Jack barked over his radio, his voice rough with anger. "Don't make this worse on yourself, Slater."

Benjamin went on as if Jack hadn't spoken. "You like bad boys like me, don't you, Officer Erica?"

Erica's cheeks flushed hotly. "I like *catching* bad boys like you."

"What do you want to do when you catch me?"

How could she answer that question? She hesitated. "I'm one of the good guys, Slater. I want to lock you up."

"Good *girl*, you mean," Benjamin said. "You want to be a good girl, right?"

Erica licked her bottom lip. "Yes." Her voice was hoarse. "I want to be a good girl."

Ben was getting in her head. He had always been good at that. He had a natural charisma, a kind of charm that was irresistible and dangerous, like a snake always ready to strike. His voice was wending its way around her thoughts, teasing her imagination. She wanted to keep him talking to prove she was a good officer, but she was getting turned on. She remembered how he tasted, how he felt moving inside her. She had never deluded herself into thinking he might care for her, but the sex had been incredible. Now, it made her hot to know she was the only one who had a little bit of power over him. Only her.

"Mmm... Then you'd better keep me happy, Erica," Ben said. "If you keep me happy, I'll give you what you want."

His words hung in the air between Erica and Jack, a double entendre that made her clench her thighs together. She looked at Jack. His face was flushed from anger. Or was it something more?

"Slater?"

"I bet you're just dying for it, aren't you?" Ben responded.

She tried to keep her voice even. "Dying for what?"

"Dying to catch me." He paused. "Or are you dying for something else, little Erica? Dying to be spanked and fucked? I'll do you so good, baby—"

"Shut up!" Erica was breathing hard, his words conjuring up memories she didn't want to think about. "Knock it off or I'm gone."

"Fine, baby. Have it your way."

The radio went silent. Jack looked at her. "What did you do that for?"

Erica resented his tone. "You heard him. That was disgusting."

"You're working, Jeffries. Don't take it personally."

She opened her mouth to ask how else she should take it when she noticed Jack's erection. She looked away, heat rising in her cheeks. Jack Randolph—her straight-laced, by-the-book partner—was aroused. The thought did something to her insides. She brushed it away, blamed it on Ben Slater. She was tired and hungry. Ben was gone, Jack was pissed at her, their shift was over and the bad guy was still out there. She just wanted to go home and go to bed. A little voice taunted her that it would be a long, long time before she fell asleep, but she ignored that, too.

She heard Jack on the radio with the other units, then the captain. Everything was a blur with only the illuminated highway signs to break up the dark, unrelenting highway landscape.

"We're going in," Jack said. "There's an APB out for him from here to the state line. Hopefully he'll slip up and someone will nail him. There's not much more we can do tonight."

"So we just give up then?"

Jack shrugged. "We can't win them all. My bet is he'll stay in the area. He's shown his weakness."

Jack didn't have to say it. Erica knew *she* was now Ben's weakness.

They pulled into the station parking lot thirty minutes later, but it was another hour before they had finished their paperwork and were able to leave for the night. She got home on autopilot, barely conscious enough to nudge the front door closed behind her. Too late, she realized she wasn't alone. Before she could even raise her hands in self defense, she was grabbed from behind and thrown down on the couch.

She swallowed the scream in her throat as she looked up at Ben Slater standing over her. He wore jeans and a black leather jacket over a dark T-shirt. A silver medallion hung on a chain around his neck, glinting in the lamplight. His eyes were nearly as dark as his jacket, the pupils blending into the irises, giving him a feral quality that hinted at suppressed rage. His hair brushed his shoulders, a black mane blending into his dark clothes. He looked like a wild man—or a man on the edge.

"Don't scream," he said. "I don't want to have to knock you around."

He didn't have a gun, but Erica had no doubt he could inflict an awful lot of damage on her body with his bare hands. She swallowed the scream in her throat and willed herself to breathe slowly.

"That's good, baby," he said, sitting beside her on the sofa. "I can't stop thinking about you. Did you think I wouldn't remember you?"

She swallowed hard. Trying not to betray her careening emotions, she asked, "Remember what?"

"Remember what a bad, bad girl you used to be. I remembered you as soon as I saw that red hair. Slut red."

"How—how did you find me?"

His laugh was low and cruel. "Didn't they tell you in the academy not to have a listed number? You're in the phone book, baby."

She was breathing hard now. She couldn't help it. Her mind, fuzzy with exhaustion a moment ago, was racing. What should she do? Should she try to get away? Overpower him?

"Don't do it," Ben warned. "I know you're weighing your options. Don't."

It startled her that he could read her so easily. He looked like the same bad boy her mother had warned her about. She could do this, she knew him. She could talk to him.

"I've been thinking about you, too."

He glanced at her, wary mistrust giving way to masculine pride. "You have?"

She nodded. She licked her dry lips and heard his sharp intake of breath. "I was thinking about what you said, about how I like bad boys. You were right." She looked at him from under her lashes, the shyness only partly an act. "I just couldn't really say anything with my partner in the car."

"That's what I thought," Benjamin grunted. "You may act like a good girl and dress like a cop now, but you still like it dirty."

"Yeah," she said. She tried to convince herself she was only going along with what he said in order to lull him. That it was just an act. "I missed you."

"I like your hair short. You look like a tough little thing now, not all girly-girl."

Self-consciously, she ran her hand through her hair. She could tell it was sticking up all over her head. "Thanks. It's a mess," she said. "I need a shower."

He reached out to touch her. "I'd like to see you dripping wet."

"No!" Without thinking, she jerked away.

His expression hardened as he stood up and strode to the door. "That's what I thought. You just want to bust me."

"Wait!" she called softly. "It wasn't that at all. Please, don't go."

He hesitated, hand on the doorknob. "How was it, then?"

Something—that bad girl from long ago—made her look him in the eye and say, "Come here and I'll show you."

He was on her in a flash, kissing her roughly, his stubble scratching her cheeks as his tongue slipped between her lips. She knew she should resist, but she couldn't. She didn't *want* to. She leaned into him, feeling his cock press against her, already hard and ready. So ready. She moaned into his mouth as she shamelessly rubbed against him. God help her, she wanted him.

Ben pulled away, dragging her toward the bedroom. Then he spun her around to face the bed. She couldn't think. She could barely breathe.

"No!" she protested, but she didn't mean it. "Ben, please."

"Please, what?" His hands groped at her utility belt, stripping it off her quicker than she could have. "Please what, baby?"

His hands were ripping at her uniform, popping the buttons on her shirt and pulling back the Velcro straps of her vest. He slid his hands underneath to squeeze her breasts through her flimsy bra, but he didn't linger long. His hands glided along her narrow waist to unfasten her uniform pants, tugging them down over her hips in one rough motion, along with her panties.

"Bend over, baby. You've been a bad girl."

She gasped as he bent her over the bed and kicked her legs apart. Her pants were down around her ankles, her heavy work boots preventing her from slipping them off. She was utterly helpless, her heart beating a frantic tattoo behind her breastbone, the taste of anticipation sweet on her tongue.

There was no rational thought in her mind as she told him what she wanted. What she needed. "Fuck me, Ben."

"I will, baby. I will."

She felt his hand on her hip and braced herself for his cock. Instead, he slapped her upturned bottom. Hard. She gasped but did not pull away. The next slap was harder and she moaned. Warmth spread across her ass and her clit tingled with every smack of his hand. He spanked her mercilessly, alternating between each cheek until she was whimpering from the exquisite pain and unbearable arousal. Her skin was on fire but her pussy felt empty and aching.

When he paused, she whispered again for him to fuck her, but her mouth was dry and the words were silent in her throat. Instead of entering her, he knelt and spread her fevered bottom, blowing his hot breath over her pussy and asshole. It was humiliating and arousing at the same time. She whimpered and was rewarded with the soft, wet stroke of his tongue.

"You taste so good," he murmured.

She whimpered again. "More, Ben."

He licked her in long, slow strokes, his tongue teasing her until every nerve ending quivered in anticipation. She pressed against his mouth, willing him to push his tongue into her. Then he did and the sensation was like nothing she had remembered. He slapped her thigh and her eyes fluttered open from the suddenness of the sting.

She realized then that her bedroom window was open, and that must have been how Ben had gained access to her house. Night was falling, but it wasn't so dark that she couldn't make out the man standing outside her window. She caught her breath, not from what Ben was doing to her this time, but from realizing who was watching them.

Jack stared at her through her open bedroom window; stared,

not with disapproval, but with a hunger so raw and fierce she could almost feel it across the distance that separated them. She gasped, orgasm rippling from her clit to her pussy to her ass, spiraling through her overheated body as she screamed out her release while Jack watched.

"I need to fuck you, baby," Ben growled.

"Yes, god, yes," she moaned, looking at Jack. Talking to Jack.

Ben stood up, releasing her for only a moment as he unzipped his pants. She never moved. She stood there, braced for him to fuck her while her partner watched silently from outside. She didn't know what road she was on anymore or where it would take her, but she knew she had to see it to the finish.

With one hand on her hip and the other guiding his cock, Ben rubbed the broad head of his erection between her legs. She moaned and pushed back against him, taking all of him inside her.

"So wet, so tight." He fucked her roughly, driving into her with such force she had to stretch out over the bed to take it.

"Fuck me hard," she moaned. The words were said to Ben, but they were meant for Jack.

"You want it harder, baby?"

"Yes, yes!"

She groaned like a wild thing as he held on to her hips and gave her what she wanted. She bit her lip to quiet herself, but he seemed intent on wringing every sound from her that he could. He gripped her short hair in his fist and pulled her head back before biting her neck. The sensation of his mouth on her neck and his cock in her pussy and Jack bearing witness to it all sent her over the edge again.

She came, screaming his name.

"Jack!"

"Oh, fuck," Ben groaned, oblivious to her mistake. "I'm gonna come, baby."

"Yes, yes, yes," she moaned, still trembling as her pussy rippled around his cock.

A moment later he tensed and went still against her as he came. His cock pulsed and she instinctively squeezed her muscles, wrenching another tortured groan from him. Finally, slowly, his cock softened inside her. Her pussy felt sore and stretched when he finally moved away.

She collapsed on the bed, her body still throbbing with the intensity of her orgasm. Suddenly, everything came rushing back: where she was, who she was with.

Jack.

She jerked up. Jack had disappeared from the window. Was he gone? Would he be crashing through the door in a minute? She had no idea of his intentions, couldn't begin to predict what he might do in this crazy situation. Or what would happen to her when the dust settled.

"I gotta get out of here, baby. But that was fun." Ben was pulling on his pants, his cock still glistening with their passion.

"Yeah," she muttered wearily. Her knees still felt like rubber as she stood, refastening her vest before pulling her shirt back on. She yanked up her pants as Ben turned toward the door.

"You're not going to call the police on me, are you?" He laughed. "Oh, wait, you *are* the police."

Whatever desire she'd felt for him had fled. Now her brain was alert, looking for an opportunity.

He gave her that familiar smirk, but his face was tired and resigned. "I'm heading to Canada. I'd ask you to come, but I know you won't. You're not that kind of girl."

"No, I'm not," she whispered as he turned to the front door.

Jack had been right. She was Ben's weakness. She followed him to the front door, biding her time. When his hand was on the doorknob, she made her move.

She had him on the ground, a knee in the small of his back, before he could even struggle. The door swung inward and Jack walked in, surveying the scene with cool professionalism as if he hadn't just watched the two of them fucking.

"Hey, partner," Erica said. "Glad you could join us."

"What the fuck!" Ben bucked, attempting to dislodge her, but she already had the cuffs on him. "I thought we were cool."

She hauled him to his feet, taking perverse pleasure in hearing him gasp as the cuffs ratcheted tighter on his wrists. "Oh, we're cool, Ben. Real cool. And you're under arrest."

"I have the squad car. I'll read him his rights and take him in." Jack took Ben by the arm and led him out the front door. "Meet you at the station?"

She nodded. "Yeah. I need a shower."

Jack cocked an eyebrow but didn't say anything.

"If you want, we'll talk when this is over." She leaned against the door frame, feeling suddenly weary after the adrenaline rush.

"I definitely want," Jack said, nearly jerking Ben off his feet as he pulled him off the porch.

"So do I," she whispered as her past and her present walked away. "So do I."

WHORE
COMPLEX

Rachel Kramer Bussel

Adrian tossed the cash on the hotel room dresser, fanning the fourteen twenties out; we both watched the crisp, green currency land against the sleek glass. My pussy gave an involuntary spasm as I saw the bills. I left them there, liking the way they decorated the room, what they symbolized, as I got down on my knees. He moved to stroke my long, just-blown-out, deep brown hair before thinking better of it and grabbing a handful, pulling me tight against his crotch.

When I moved to kiss his hardness through his jeans, he said, "I'm not paying you to kiss me." Fuck, but that made me gasp. I looked up at him through the layers of my false eyelashes, at the Hawaiian-print red and orange shirt stretched across his bulky body and his pale brown eyes staring back at me, before I unzipped him and took his half-hard cock into my mouth. The truth is, I'd pay *him* for this opportunity, especially to feel him getting even harder as I went about my business.

I shut my eyes to better focus on the exquisite sensation of having him in my mouth, of being full of him, smelling him, tasting him, reveling in him, until he made me open my eyes to watch his cock as it slid in and out of my lips. That went on until he needed to come, and almost as if he were angry at me for making the blow job end, he pulled out and lashed his cock across my face. "Take it," he said, shoving himself back inside me, his voice going hoarse, his body starting to shake as I did what he told me to, my own body coming alive as I curved my mouth around him. When he came inside me, there was so much of it I had trouble swallowing, but I did, somehow, then stayed there, wrapped around him, his hand on my head, our bodies entwined.

I'm not really a whore, though I am his whore; I even bought him a card that proclaimed as much, though I keep it tucked away in my desk drawer, only to be spied when I go to get a paper clip or envelope, a reminder I in no way need because I live and breathe my whoredom every second of the day. While some men pay real whores for "the girlfriend experience," I gave up my girlfriend life for this one long ago. The first time Adrian said it to me I was pinned underneath him, his hefty arms locking mine in place. "Don't ever forget that you're my whore," he said, before leaning down to bite my cheek, clamping down at the fleshy rounded-apple pouf of my face, the part magazines tell you to sweep the blush brush over. I liked it at first, the bite, liked that he was literally sinking his teeth into me, indulging in me like he would a fine steak.

Then he bit me again in the same place before coming up so his lips were just above mine. His hand closed around my neck, forcing my eyes up and into his. "That means I can do anything I want to you, any time."

He wasn't asking me a question but I could sense he needed me to respond, to confirm the truth of his statement. "Yes,"

I said, simple and direct, even though the single syllable still managed to get caught in my throat. What was I really agreeing to? I wouldn't know until later, but from the first time he'd beckoned me to sit on his lap and whispered that he'd thought about me stripping for him before he bent me over and held me down, I knew I'd agree to anything. His voice ricocheted against my skin, vibrating against my ear, echoing in my memory. We were just verbally agreeing to what I'd consented to that day months ago.

Since then I've learned that being a private whore requires a lot of upkeep. It's not just the visits to the gym, hairdresser, waxer, dermatologist and other maintenance. It's dressing the part; I can't exactly wear micro-miniskirts and dresses slit up to just below my ass to my editorial job at a top magazine, even if our beat is fashion. I have a section of my closet that I think of as Adrian's, since I only wear these outfits for him. Some of them are ones he's given me, the most obscene, short and slutty, of course. Once, when I balked at a see-through pale pink dress I was sure had been marketed as a nightie, he told me he wouldn't see me if I refused to wear it. Thinking I was clever, I wore two lacy white slips beneath it. He'd made me wait at the hotel bar, nursing my margarita until I was forced to order another, enduring the stares, leers and come-ons of countless horny businessmen, until he finally strode in. Upon seeing that I had layered myself up, that my nipples were not actually visible through the garment—though I figured they were close enough since they were hard and jutting forward—he promptly walked up to me, whispered in my ear, "You are obviously terrible at listening to orders. Maybe I picked the wrong girl, after all," then reached up and pinched my inner thigh hard enough to make me wince, before walking out. I had to pay for my drinks and leave casually enough that it didn't look like I was following him, while

absorbing the last few, "I'd pay for a piece of *that*," comments
as I hobbled along in my five-inch heels. By the time I emerged
from the bar he was long gone and if I knew him, he was already
moving in on that evening's piece of ass, one who wouldn't hesitate to submit to any of his demands. He didn't answer my calls
or emails, and I wound up checking into a room, too upset to
even masturbate.

When he finally got back to me the next day, it was to berate
me. "If you are truly serious about being my whore, you have
to forget about what *you* want, and focus on what I tell you. If
you're not interested, you can go off and find someone who'll
put up with your bullshit, but I won't." He didn't need to tell
me that he already had a wife, that I was merely his plaything,
albeit one who was very good at sucking his cock. I knew that
was my ace in the hole but he sounded convincing enough that I
wasn't sure if the line I'd crossed was truly irreversible. I vowed
to myself to rededicate myself to him, writing *WHORE* over
and over in my journal, scrawling it across my inner arm, staring
at the word on my skin long enough to let it seep into my mind
before I washed it off.

For our date the following weekend, he had his friend Janet,
who runs a high-end clothing store, dress me. She made sure
to let drop that she knew all about what was going on with
us, mentioning our "arrangement" as she slid thigh-high fishnet
stockings up my legs and paired them with a sixties-inspired
Pucci-print orange, pink and white dress that stopped just at my
upper thighs, meaning I wouldn't be able to sit without exposing
my panties...except she told me he'd forbidden me to wear
panties. My cheeks burned; sure, I often went sans underwear
for him, but this stranger was chatting about that fact as casually
as she might comment on the tiny birthmark on my ass, which
I'm sure she'd seen as I changed since she'd insisted on entering

the tiny cubicle with me. This led me to wonder whether he'd told her everything about us, from how much I loved to have his belt wrapped around my throat to how we'd let the white-haired room service deliveryman watch me give him an extended blow job in lieu of a tip.

When Janet's fingers brushed against my pussy, at first I didn't know if it was an accident. I tried to move away but her grip on my wrist tightened as her fingers probed farther. "Adrian told me to make sure you were ready for him," she said right there in her dressing room, her fingers snaking inside my pussy. I wanted to ask if I should take the dress off first but apparently not, because Janet was soon coaxing my G-spot out of hiding. I could have protested, but not only did she know what she was doing, I knew what I was doing, too: obeying. Even when I was doing something I might never have chosen to do, obeying got me wetter than I'd ever been even with guys I'd been oh-so-serious with, the ones I'd thought were so good in bed. If only I'd known what I was missing. It wasn't just disappointing Adrian that had upset me; it was that I hadn't gotten the rewards that always come with doing as he says.

Janet pushed me against the wall so I could see us in the mirror. Me, with my honey blonde hair piled atop my head in an artfully arranged bun, my suntanned skin dotted with freckles, the colorful dress bunched around my waist as this wisp of a woman twisted her fingers inside me. Immediately I started to wonder whether they'd been lovers, whether he'd watched her with other women, whether he'd told her exactly how to fuck me. Then I stopped wondering anything because Janet, whether she was following orders or not, clearly had a vested interest in making me come: her mouth had found its way to my clit. I heard her say something, though I couldn't make out the words since my breathing was so loud in my ears. Her quick exhalations were warm against me, and I braced my arms above my head against the wall as I pushed down against her invading digits and probing tongue. The more I let myself go, the more fully she occupied me, adding another digit, nipping at my clit, mashing her face into me. My orgasm overtook me and I shook against the wall, worried I'd fall to the floor.

Janet smiled at me when she was done, rising and winking at me, not even hinting that I return the favor, though I'd gladly have done so. "I can see why he wants you," she said before kissing me, granting me a taste of my flavor on her lips. "I think you're ready for him now," she said.

"What do I owe you?" I asked, fumbling for my purse, startled by the sudden sense of intimacy I felt between us. It was one thing to fuck under orders, another to feel myself wanting to kiss her deeper, longer, in ways that had nothing to do with Adrian. I wasn't used to my attention being diverted from him, but he was always finding new ways to keep me on my toes.

"It's on the house," she said, before leaning down to bite me in the exact spot that was still just a little sore from the last time I'd seen Adrian. Did he bite every woman there? Was that his trademark? Janet was gentler than he usually was, her teeth merely grazing my skin, but it was clear she knew exactly how tender I was there.

I couldn't ask her any of the questions bubbling up in me, partly because I had to go meet him, partly because it wouldn't have been appropriate. "Are you a member of the secret whores club?" didn't exactly roll off a girl's lips—even mine. So I walked out, sure that everything I'd just done was as obvious to all as the fact that I was going commando.

Adrian had made me promise to walk to the hotel. It was only five blocks, and I'm a New Yorker and therefore a dedicated power walker, but I'm usually in my tricked-out sneakers, not tottering heels and a dress that, with one slight breeze, could have me committing an act of obscenity. I held my spine straight, seeing the world anew with the added height, and glad I'd opted for only the lightest of purses. I wondered what a real whore would wear on a date; I figured she'd probably take a cab and get changed there. I could have cheated, but somehow he would find out. Once, he'd made me promise to make myself come, and I'd fallen asleep before I had a chance and I didn't have it in me to lie to him. He'd taken his belt and lashed it directly against my pussy. "Thank you, I'm sorry," I repeated until the words sounded robotic, my tender sex was sore and tears were streaming down my face. "Now make yourself come for me," he'd responded and even though I was in pain, I managed to slide my fingers inside myself and do as he'd asked. While I touched myself, he dangled the belt against my lips, brushed it against my cheeks, tapped it against my breasts, until I trembled in and out and out and in, and he held me in his arms while I came.

It wasn't a matter of it being worth it or not, it just was. "Everything happens for a reason," he said then, leaving out the part where the reason was so often for him to know and me to never find out. Being his whore wasn't about money so much as possession, submission, subjugation. Being his whore meant that I had to trust him even when every instinct told me not to. I focused on that word *whore* as I took each step toward him.

At the start, he'd told me that my life would go on as usual; I'd simply be available to him when he needed me. That was the only untruth he'd told me since we started our relationship. There was no way I could be his whore and be someone else's anything; maybe another girl could've pulled off that trick, but not me. Being his whore was everything to me. It meant I thought of him while I spread my legs at the spa and got my pussy waxed, wishing he were there to watch, to see me in pain, which he so enjoyed. It meant that every man—the ones who flirted shamelessly with me, the ones I was tempted to kiss, the ones I sometimes did grab and tongue-fuck in a corner of some party—was compared to him in my mind and left wanting.

When I walked into the lobby, Adrian was sitting and sipping from a small glass of amber liquid, reading the newspaper. I walked toward him, willing him to look up at me, but he refused, though I knew he saw me; he always does. I walked straight up to him and then only merited a quick flicking of his eyes up and down my body. I blushed despite myself, feeling a chill against my bare legs. "Can I help you?" he asked.

"I..." I paused, uncertain what to say. I'd been expecting him to do what he usually does, try to get as much PDA in as he can before I squirm and he takes pity on me. I hadn't expected to have to beg for his attention.

"We have a date," I said quietly, suddenly uncertain. I stole a glance around but there was just the staff going about their business, a few guests checking in, one man in a suit rifling through a *New York Times*.

"I don't have a date scheduled with anyone, sorry," he said, his voice louder than necessary—ruder, too. I struggled not to cry; here I was, dressed in a way no sane woman would dress, my pussy practically exposed, not to mention wet from being so near him, and he was pushing me away. "You should take your business elsewhere, *ma'am*," he said, the last word filled with as much hostility as he possessed. His eyes stared blankly back at me. What could I do? I could hardly sit down in the dress without wetting the seat, not to mention exposing myself, without even a sweater to drape over my lap.

I noticed the man in the suit staring at me and I offered him a tepid smile. His head jerked almost imperceptibly, but I caught it. He thought I was a real whore! Or just easy. I tottered over to him, aware the whole time of Adrian's eyes on me. "Hello there," he said, his voice dripping with Texas charm. "What's a pretty girl like you doing in my neck of the woods?" he asked, then laughed at his non-joke.

There was a seat next to him but he motioned to his lap, as if that's what people did in the middle of the day in fancy hotels— sat on each other's laps. I was already so mixed up I figured I might as well go with it, so I did, gingerly placing myself across his lap, my legs together, the dress doing an impressive job of covering me just enough. He shifted his paper so it covered my upper thighs, and he rested his fingers between them. My heart pounded, but when I looked over at Adrian, he just gave me an enigmatic smile. Was this man another of his minions, like Janet? The man's hands, despite my clamped-together thighs, somehow made their way to my pussy. He had to have felt my wet heat through his pants even before his fingers found me out. "How much, sugar?" he asked as he touched me lightly.

I opened my mouth but just looked at him. Up close, he wasn't bad looking, not my type, but hot enough, with slightly graying hair and a leathery face that had obviously spent plenty of time in the sun. His eyes were a deep blue and seemed amused by my predicament. "I'm not..." I started to say, but he *tsked* at me.

"I know exactly what you are," he said, his voice low and a little mean. "The question is, how much is it going to cost me to have those pretty little lips wrapped around my cock?"

My heart started pounding then; it was one thing to play at being a whore for Adrian, when I felt indebted to him for granting me access to his glorious body, his razor-sharp mind. But this man was someone I'd never give a second glance, would hardly have let buy me drinks under normal circumstances. And that's when it sank in, once and for all: being Adrian's whore had nothing to do with "normal."

"I know you're for sale, sweetheart. Word gets around." He didn't need to say Adrian's name to let me know what he meant. Adrian had set this up, but whether this man was a friend, a business acquaintance, or just someone he'd discovered in the lobby, I didn't know. If I were a real whore, I'd be making money off this transaction, but it wasn't the money that motivated me. It was Adrian watching me, judging me. I'd fucked up once and wasn't going to again, since this had to be a test. But how much to charge? I raked my memory for Julia Roberts in *Pretty Woman* but could only come up with her singing Prince in the bath and shopping on Rodeo Drive.

"A thousand. Full service," I said, the words emerging from some part of me I hadn't known existed. *Full service?* WTF? But once I'd said it, I couldn't take it back, especially when my legs parted apparently just enough for his fingers to sink all the way into my cunt.

"That's a lot of money for a working girl," he said. "I hope you're worth it. I like it rough," he said right into my ear. I shut my eyes for a moment because I couldn't quite believe what was happening. I was dying for Adrian's hands on me, his belt, his kiss, his cock, but instead I was sitting on a strange Texan's lap while he fingered me, in a designer dress in the middle of a daytime hotel lobby. "Get up," he said, easing his fingers out and the paper off of us while I did my best to rise without causing a scene.

When I looked where Adrian had been sitting, he was gone. What if I was wrong and he didn't actually know this man? To ask would surely be to breach etiquette, and by now I kind of wanted the cash. One thousand dollars is a lot of money, never mind that I have a decent corporate job and didn't strictly need it. I could find plenty of uses for a quick grand. His hand rested on my lower back, just above my ass, pushing me forward, as if sensing my second thoughts. A bellhop rolled a luggage cart over just as the elevator dinged, and the three of us entered. "What floor?" he asked, turning first to me and then, seeing as I had no answer, to my companion.

"Twenty-three," the Texan said, and the bellhop pressed that for us, followed by thirty. An elevator ride at a hotel like that should have taken a minute at the most, but it seemed to take forever, especially when the man's hand slid from its resting spot to between my legs. I couldn't help the small gasp that escaped my lips, and my eyes met the bellhop's. He stared blatantly, almost hungrily, and I wondered if my client would dare to raise my skirt. Instead he pushed me toward the bellhop. I didn't say a word, reminding myself I was doing this not for either of them, but for Adrian. The numbers were rising so he didn't have much time, but the bellhop was good; in just two floors he had three fingers inside me, staring into my eyes while he probed, pressing the front of his pants down with his other hand to show me how hard he was. The bell dinged and Mr. Texas said, "Come to room twenty-three-oh-seven in an hour and you can have her," before pulling me away from the elevator.

"He deserves a treat, don't you think?" he asked before tugging me along toward the room. I tried to keep my thoughts firmly on Adrian, to get myself properly in the mood.

The man slipped the card into the hole and when the green light blinked, pushed it open, and I followed. He had a large suite, with two enormous beds, a giant TV, DVD player and stereo. A bottle of champagne sat chilling on ice. He took a cube and traced it over my lips, then ran it along my neck before pushing me back against the bed. I sat up and said, "I need my money."

I'd never had to ask a man for money like that before; it felt strange, exhilarating yet very, very wrong. It would be one thing if I would have fucked him anyway, but I wouldn't, I knew that. Even if he had a giant cock, even if he knew how to hit me just right, I wouldn't have voluntarily joined him in bed, at least not without copious amounts of alcohol or a really hot trophy wife on his arm. His hand went around my neck, hard enough that I could feel he'd done it before and knew his way around choking girls. He pulled his wallet out of his pants then straddled me, his legs on either side of my chest as he tossed the bills onto me, counting out ten hundreds before shoving them off the bed and onto the floor. He unzipped his pants and pulled out his cock. If Adrian had been watching, I'd have been thrilled to open up. He likes to tell me that I'm so hungry for cock I probably want to suck every man who crosses my path...and he's not far off. I don't actually do it, but I do think about who's well-endowed, who'd give me trouble, who'd take delight in face-fucking me.

But Adrian was not here, and this man whose name I still didn't know was, with his insistent hard-on right in front of me. I wasn't repulsed, but as I took it into my mouth, it wasn't with the same hunger as when I sucked Adrian. I shut my eyes and tried to focus, to give him his money's worth, and that was what made me wet, the knowledge that as much as I may have been a devoted whore to Adrian, I was truly a whore for this man, and a well-paid one. I sucked him the way I would a man I was in love with, the way I would Adrian, and soon, with his fat, long cock stuffing my mouth, I found myself eager for all of him, wanting not just to suck him but to devour him. I wondered if this was all he wanted as I rolled the tip of my tongue along his length. He pulled back, then slammed his dick into my mouth, his legs resting against the sides of my face. I didn't know him one iota, didn't know a thing about him except that he could afford this, and that was all I needed to know.

He fucked my face for a few minutes and just when I thought he might come, he pulled back and held my throat tight—again, like Adrian, but different. He had bought my body but not my soul, after all. He slapped my face and I smiled up at him. "I heard you like that," he said before hitting me on the same cheek, harder. I blushed, an absurdity under the circumstances, but I couldn't help it—Adrian had told him about what sets me off, about what we do together.

The man got up and beckoned me to stand, as well, before slipping a blindfold over my eyes. He bent me over the bed and tied something around my wrists. "You'll be quiet, won't you? Because otherwise I'll have to gag you," he said. I nodded, suddenly scared; there'd be no way to call for help if that happened, but I had to trust Adrian and, therefore, trust him. "I'm going to give you twenty spankings, and then I'm going to fuck you, and I want you to stay perfectly still. If you move, I'm going to have to start over."

I nodded even though he probably wasn't looking at my face, couldn't see my chin move into the pillow. I wasn't nodding to him, anyway, but to myself, to Adrian. I wanted him so badly by then, to hear his familiar, sexy voice so low and knowing and intimate, just for me, the one that always layered even the most painful punishment with a soothing aural caress. I thought the man was going to spank me with his hand, which I could totally handle, but he had a belt. "You might recognize this," he said after the first blow struck me hard, and I knew: he was using Adrian's belt, yet it felt different, and I realized that he could hit me as hard as he wanted, but it was never going to feel like it did with Adrian.

That didn't mean it didn't hurt—nor that I didn't like it.

I thanked him and counted after each one, and found myself getting wetter and wetter, the familiar instrument becoming one with my body, reacquainting itself with my ass and upper thighs. The heels of my white shoes dug firmly into the carpet as the familiar fire of the belt swept along my backside. I didn't cry or move, but I wasn't stoic; I just let my pussy respond for me; my mind I saved for Adrian. To give this man that would mean I'd have to forfeit being Adrian's, would mean I'd sacrificed a slice of my title to the highest bidder.

He didn't try to talk to me as he hit me, and I didn't try to figure him out the way I did with Adrian. When his cock sank into me, I welcomed it with my wetness, even let him turn me over and kiss me. He took off the blindfold, and we shared a moment that went beyond money. Even though he wasn't literally in the room with us, I felt Adrian smiling down at me. I lifted my legs, wrapped them around the man's back and squeezed my pussy muscles, needing to give him the best fuck I could. I wondered if Adrian had told him to wear a condom; either way, I was glad he was wearing one, because I only wanted Adrian's come in me.

He sank down onto me after he'd come, then kissed me gently. I saw a little bit of who he was then, opening my eyes while his were closed. My curiosity briefly sparked, but I pushed it aside. A knock sounded at the door and he got up and put on his jeans, and I stood, wishing for even a thong to pull up, but had to settle for tugging my dress down instead.

He opened the door and there stood the bellhop...and Adrian. The freckled, boyish man in a suit with his five o'clock shadow sprouting just looked at us, and Texas ushered him inside while he put his clothes back on and handed me an extra hundred and smiled at me. I tossed it on the floor with the others, offering a smile to the bellhop even as my heart leapt at seeing Adrian.

The Texan slipped out but not without passing the belt to Adrian. They did that man thing of patting each other on the shoulder before he walked out. I thought I heard him whistling. "Go ahead, Claire, give him what he was promised." Did my man know everything? Suddenly I was shy, perhaps because the bellhop seemed to be as well. He was young, twenty or younger, and I realized I'd have to get things started. "I think he wants to know how good a cocksucker you are, Claire," Adrian said.

Now the man knew my name. And Adrian was about to watch me do something he'd never seen me do with another man. I looked up at him but he just stared at me again with that same blank look he'd offered in the lobby. I pulled the dress off and tossed it and my bra onto the pile of money. The bellhop grinned at me and said, "Pretty," in a quiet, sweet voice. I had thought I'd be into Adrian watching me, but I had to pretend he wasn't there, pretend I was some Mrs. Robinson type seducing a man young enough to, technically, be my son.

"Touch her," Adrian said, and the man who'd been so lewd in the elevator reverently stroked my breasts, his fingers passing over my nipple piercing with awe, pausing over it, his thumb caressing the silver end of the dumbbell. "She has another one on her clit," Adrian said, and the boy moved his hand lower, then again dipped his fingers into me. I was still wet, and I let myself go in a way I hadn't with the Texan, the people pleaser in me wanting everyone to get off. "Come for him, Claire, show him what it feels like." I didn't really want to come for him; I wanted to come with Adrian inside me, holding me down, telling me what a good whore I was.

But I knew I wouldn't get that if I didn't listen to him, so I arched up to meet the manboy's fingers, tentative at first and then less so. I pulled him close for a kiss. He tasted like coffee and mint, and I ran my fingers through the fuzz on his head.

We tumbled around on the bed for a while and then just when I thought it might never happen, his fingers curled and pressed and found what they were looking for, and I shuddered in his arms. He pulled out and sucked on his fingers, then offered them to me.

I reached down, felt how hard he was and took out his cock, pushing his pants down. I showed it to Adrian, wrapping my hand around it, and he walked over and poured some lube for me. I stroked the second man whose name I wouldn't know as we all watched my hand twisting around, my thumb sliding along the tip. "Yes, yes," he said, "please," and then a mishmash of words I couldn't identify except for their urgency. Adrian pressed my head down when he started thrashing, and I took it in my mouth and almost immediately felt him spurt inside me. Adrian held me there, silently commanding me to suck every drop.

"That's a good whore," he said, easing me up and kissing me while the younger man just watched, his eyes wide, before getting up and going to the bathroom to wash up. When he came out, Adrian said, "Tip him," and somehow, that act made me feel the most whore-like of all. I was giving a man fifty bucks for making me come and letting me suck his cock, when I hadn't even wanted him involved at all. He stared at the tip for a moment, unsure of what to do, then took it, said, "Thank you," and kissed me on the cheek before leaving.

Adrian took out the collar he'd bought for me and fastened it around my neck, attaching the chain he likes to use to tug me around, pulling it tight. "A good whore learns from her mistakes," he said before yanking open the curtains and pushing me against the glass so that all of Chelsea that cared to look would see my body pressed against its surface while he unfurled the belt. And he was right: I didn't protest once while he beat me, the belt tracing familiar lines along my ass. All I did was steam up the window in gratitude at having passed his test, waiting for whatever was coming next, because I'd learned from Adrian that good whores don't just learn from their mistakes, they also get rewarded for them.

LESSONS, SLOW AND PAINFUL

Tess Danesi

I look forward to the weekends, especially at this time of year when the weather is somewhere between summer and autumn. The cool apple crispness of morning warmed by the sun to a mellow golden heat in the afternoon transforms again to a chilly evening, a chill that almost persuades me to order one of those awful Snuggies for when the ochre hue of October metamorphoses into the frigid steel gray of November. This Saturday finds Dar in his office at seven a.m. Not an unusual occurrence by any means, though I'd prefer to be in Dar's over-sized bed, heat radiating from his chest warming my back, his cock stirring and hardening as he wakes, his breath gentle and steady on my neck, his voice, dark and thick with sleep, whispering sweet obscenities in my ear. Yes, I'd prefer that any day of the week.

Though this morning is not to be one of those days, it seems a glorious day. The early morning sunlight streams through my open bedroom curtains. I'm not sure if it was the brilliant, white light or Diablo's soft little tongue licking my face that woke me. But I'm up and feel invigorated by the lovely day, so I shower quickly, throw on a pair of black leggings, a tunic and a pair of kitten-heeled black suede boots that come up over my knees, and grab a sweater. I rattle Diablo's leash, which sends him scurrying, slipping and sliding along the hardwood floors with excitement. I make sure I have his carrying case to double as my handbag. I got the leopard print one, succumbing to the rolling of Dar's eyes when I'd picked up a pink one. My intended destination is Union Square. I plan to hit DSW to salivate and drool all over the newest fall shoes and boots. Hopefully, using some restraint, I'll even purchase a few pairs.

I emerge from the subway at Union Square, seeing a buzz of activity despite the early hour. It's the farmer's market. I had forgotten, but now thoughts of shoes are almost—almost— replaced by the sensuality of the market. Its rich colors, spicy scents, picture-perfect displays of fruits and vegetables and bazaarlike feel remind me that I raced out without even a cup of coffee. Diablo is yapping inside his case; Diablo, much like Dar, never lets me forget his presence. And there the similarities end. My dog is a little puff of unruly white fur, loquaciousness and frenzy. Dar, well, Dar is none of those things. Hard, often silent when his demons possess him, a too-frequent occurrence really, unflappable and rigid, that's Dar. Perhaps that's why I chose a pet that is so diametrically opposite my lover. Plus, it's fun to see Dar, a six-foot-three mass of lean, hard muscle, thanks to the workout regimen that he adheres to with religious fervor, walking Diablo.

First, I leash Diablo and immediately he runs frantically, pulling the cord to its maximum length, as he takes off in pursuit of a squirrel. Reeling him back in, I scoop him up, kiss his wet nose and admonish him for his naughty behavior. My next stop is at a stall for a large cup of steaming coffee. As I always do, before taking a sip, I inhale deeply, losing myself for a precious moment in the deep scent and the heat that warms my hands through the paper cup. I find a vendor selling croissants, debate for a moment whether the flaky butteriness is worth all those calories and buy one. Diablo is getting antsy, wanting to chase anything that moves, but I rein him in long enough to eat my breakfast. I rip off a couple of flaky pieces and feel his teeth snap at my fingers as he greedily grabs the pastry.

Now sated, we make our way through the stalls as I grab some gorgeous, bright red organic tomatoes; buffalo mozzarella; a huge bunch of fragrant basil; two loaves of artisanal bread, one with flecks of prosciutto; a small bottle of aged balsamic vinegar, thick and sweet; and a bottle of cold-pressed, unfiltered, organic olive oil. I feel the need to have this summery meal today, since it might well be the last time this year to enjoy such perfection. I figure I'll stop at my local liquor store and grab a nice bottle of Chianti before arranging a simple but superb lunch for Dar. Texting him to find out when he'll be done, I'm treated to a nearly instantaneous reply: *I'll see you at two at your place.*

There are no shortcuts or text speak with Dar. He texts as if writing a formal letter and hates when I lapse into LOL or, god forbid, an emoticon.

I'm so burdened by my groceries that I contemplate abandoning DSW for today, but its large sign just across the street is too much of an enticement. With Diablo ensconced in his carrier, I make my way through the narrow aisles, making a beeline for the highest heels I see, despite my promise to myself to look for some more practical footwear. Settling on a pair of kickass, utterly impractical shoes and two pairs of equally impractical boots, I pay and take the long escalator down to the street. It's such a gorgeous day that there's a proliferation of empty taxis, and I hail one in seconds and am in front of the liquor store in just over ten minutes.

Back in my apartment by noon, I put away all my purchases before taking another shower and dressing in anticipation of seeing Dar. I know the little black dress I don, draped loosely in the front with a low-cut *V* in the back, too short for street wear, will irk Dar if he thinks I wore it around town. I plan on putting on a pair of my new shoes once I have the meal prepared. And after not seeing him for several days, I feel the need to have some of his legendary temper and frustration channeled into sexual perversity. I want to be taken hard today, roughed up and left battered and bruised for my efforts. I apply extra eyeliner and nonwaterproof mascara, hoping that thick black streaks will soon be staining my face. In a perfect symbiosis, ruined beauty makes Dar's erection painfully hard, which in turn makes me even wetter and puts me in a place where time seems suspended. I crave that place.

Looking at the clock, I see it's nearly two. *Damn it. How did time get away from me?* But isn't it always that way? The more time I think I have, the more time I spend prepping and go from being early to running late in the blink of an eye. Racing to the kitchen, large enough for two people to cook together comfortably—one of the reasons I chose this apartment—I see Diablo peacefully snoozing in the sun that shines through the dining room window, his fur glistening like a fresh field of snow. I contemplate moving him to the bedroom but decide he looks too peaceful to disturb. My dog seems not to have outgrown his puppy year and can even snooze through Dar's maddeningly high-volume playing of Disturbed.

I set the table first; cheerful yellow ceramic dishes will look beautiful with bright red tomatoes, green basil and the white cheese. Crystal wineglasses add a needed touch of sparkle. I uncork the Chianti, inhale its aroma and set it down to breathe. Finally, setting up my purchases on the cutting board, I grab the large chef's knife from the block and attempt to slice a tomato.

Fuck, just what I need now, I think, as the tomato resists the dull blade. Quickly, I pull out the electric knife sharpener Dar gifted me with after seeing the condition of my knives. I am now a true believer in the beauty of a perfectly honed blade. I zip the blade along, first one side, then the next, through the first of three stages of sharpening. This one is so loud it reminds me of days long gone by when mobile knife sharpeners would ring doorbells. I wonder if I've ever actually seen that outside of a movie, and I think not. My mind is a strange place, indeed.

I never hear him enter; I'm not aware of his presence or of how long he's stood watching me, until his large hand envelopes mine.

Stepping in closer, until his chest presses against my back, his groin presses mine hard, pushing my belly into the edge of the counter. He whispers into my ear slowly, words smooth as velvet, each syllable perfectly enunciated as if to emphasize what he says.

"Have I taught you nothing, pet? How many times have I told you that sharpening knives is a slow process? And once again I find you rushing through what should be an act of reverence."

All my calm evaporates as my words flow out in a breathless stream that clearly indicates he's thrown me off guard. "I know, love, but I was just running late and then the stupid knife was dull and..."

"Quiet now, Tess, let's just do this together once again, shall we? It appears you pay little attention to my lessons, slut."

Slut. Just that one word arouses me intensely. My cunt throbs insistently as my nipples harden and press against the thin fabric of my dress. I haven't bothered with a bra or panties, and I find myself wishing Dar's hand would move from mine and slip under my dress. I want to be impaled on his thick fingers; I want him to feel this tangible evidence of my arousal before it starts dripping down my thighs. But if experience is any guide, it may be quite a while before I get my wish.

With his hand over mine, deliberately he guides the knife through each stage. The abrasively loud metallic grinding stage is brief, but the other stages feel as though they take forever, though I'm not about to complain. Maintaining the proper angle and letting the mechanism determine the speed of each pass effects a transformation in my mind. His cock is the blade, steely and unrelenting, sliding in and out of my cunt, represented by the deep grooves of the sharpener. The magnets grasping the blade become my muscles clenching at him, unwilling to release him, desperately wanting him to remain so intimately a part of me. Sharp teeth sink into my neck and jolt me out of my dreaminess.

"Pay attention to the task at hand, bitch," he snarls. And then his left hand reaches under my dress, which has already been hiked up to the edge of my bottom, violently pushing two fingers deep inside me, insuring that my attention is anywhere but on the task.

"Ffffuck, Dar, what are you trying to do to me?"

"I'm just giving you a little of what you apparently so desperately need, pet."

Still guiding my hand and the blade through the last stage of the sharpener, he says, "Nearly done. Then we can see how good of a job you did, Tess."

Dar releases my hand and with a deep breath I place the knife on the counter and try to turn to face him.

"Oh, no, pet, stay right there. You don't need to see me quite yet."

Still using his body to keep mine where he wants it, he takes the knife from where I've placed it on the counter and holds it up to the light. I feel him staring down the length of the large blade, determining if it's sharp and straight enough.

"Only one way to tell, isn't there, Tess?"

His breath feels even hotter on my neck as my skin has gone cool with fear. But fear is erotic to me, at least this kind of fear. A fear rooted in faith in Dar to hurt me, yes, but never to harm me. My emotions are so jumbled, I'm such a mass of erotic tension that I neglect to answer him. His hand reaches into my hair, snakes and twists it into a large mass of mahogany waves, and he pulls my neck back so far that I can see his eyes for the first time. Deep, chocolate brown eyes that burn with a cold fire, a fire that has singed me so many times before. More than anything, I want those flames licking my body again.

"Beg me to cut you, Tess," he whispers darkly. "Beg me, bitch."

I don't hesitate. I can't pretend that I don't want this. "Do it, Dar. Do it. Go on and just do it," I reply.

"And you expect me to do it hurriedly, Tess? I don't think so," he says, accompanied by a cruel little laugh that chills me.

His hands are on my shoulders, the dress not an obstacle, and his fingers give me goose bumps as he runs them lightly over the skin of my throat. Reaching the edge of the neckline he pulls until the dress slides off my shoulders and drops to the floor, a black pool surrounding my bare feet. I hear him open the fly of his trousers, a sound that makes me want to fall to my knees and surround his perfect cock with the warmth of my mouth. I'm so wet that he glides effortlessly inside me. And then I feel the cold steel on my back.

It's strange, but I never know if he's really cutting me or not. With my endorphins spinning out of control, my head buzzing, my thighs dripping with arousal, everything is such a jumble of sensation and wild emotion. I feel something cold and rigid tracing patterns on my back, of course, but it could be the flat top of the knife and not the blade. My body responds by tensing, my bottom tightening, squeezing around the length of him inside me, my breathing becomes deep and shallow. My voice cracks when I try to utter anything but a moan.

"You know, Tess, I believe we need to reinforce your need to slow down, not to rush around so chaotically, my beautiful, fast little bitch," he says as he pushes the chef's knife back into the block.

Reaching into the inner pocket of his jacket, he retrieves his ever-present butterfly knife.

"Another lesson, bitch," he says softly, belying his sadistic intentions. "Use the proper tools for the job."

"Dar, oh, fuck, Dar," I murmur as he rocks his hips slowly, rhythmically, each thrust leaving me more and more breathless. He stops suddenly, sliding his cock out of my needy cunt, making me moan in frustration.

His hand is suddenly between my thighs, grabbing my clit, squeezing in a way that's painful to the point of insane plea-sure. I writhe against him, pressing myself back into his erection. He releases my clit and blood floods back into it, engorging it further, and making me nearly dizzy.

"Time for that later, pet," he says, wrapping his hand in my hair again and guiding me toward the dining room table. He turns me to face him, letting me get a good look at the blade gleaming in his hand before commanding me to lie facedown on the table. His commands are usually spoken in the softest voice, devoid of emotion; it's clear that he'll broach no argu-ment and as usual, I do as he orders, though never without that frisson between desire, emotion and intellect. An intellect that right now is screaming inside me, *Are you mad, are you insane, what the hell are you doing and doing nearly joyfully?*

"Stay put," he says, walking to the bathroom, returning with alcohol and cotton, chilling me as he swabs my back.

This time, when I feel the blade against my skin, it's clear he's cut me. He does it slowly; it's painful yet bearable—until it suddenly becomes unbearable. He stops when he senses I'm at my limit. Nuzzles my neck, speaks gentle words of encouragement into my ear, reminds me of how pain is followed by pleasure. He reads my body perfectly. Though I have a safeword, I rarely have had to use it.

A strange thought leaps to my consciousness, blasting its way through the jumble of emotions and sensations. I feel as though we're playing that game I'd played as a child, where you write on someone's back with your finger and they have to guess the word. The brutally slow pace he works at confounds me as I try to guess what he may be writing. That and the pain that comes in waves, crashing hard against the shore, sending salty spray high into the air and then ebbing, make it impossible for me to venture a guess.

When he drops the knife to the table, he steps back to admire his work. "Perfect, just perfect," he says, before he soaks another cotton ball in alcohol and cleans the wounds, making me, at last, scream. My scream awakens Diablo, the worst guard dog in history, from his afternoon siesta. He bounds over to the table, spry as a mini-gazelle, yapping happily. Dar picks him up and allows him to lick his face once before placing him back on the floor.

I attempt to stand, find myself shaking and he immediately steadies me so I don't fall.

"I want to see what you did, you bastard." My bravado is a transparent cover for my fear and Dar knows it.

Inside my bedroom, I turn to the mirror and attempt to look over my shoulder but of course the words are reversed. Dar comes in and lifts the hand mirror from my dresser so I can better see his handiwork. On my lower back, right above my ass, in precise letters that still weep droplets of crimson, are the words FAST GIRL.

I shudder as I think that I allowed him to do this to me. No one but Dar could ever drive me to and make me desire such extremes. Dropping the mirror, he lifts me in his strong arms, carefully avoiding the cuts on my back and playfully tosses me on my bed, stripping the burgundy velvet coverlet off the bed beneath me. For an instant, the stinging in my lower back reminds me that I'm bleeding, and I worry about staining my crisp, white sheets and then his lips, full, soft and gentle, meet my lips.

His kiss makes the world go away.

His kiss makes it all go away.

SPEED BUMPS

Tenille Brown

Sunny checked her watch before she gripped the bars on her bike tighter, bending low to take the curve. She would be there in less than five minutes. She had been shooting for fifteen, had wanted to be very casual and nonchalant about it, but that was the thing about motorcycles; they always made you appear too eager, even when the intent was to make 'em wait awhile.

In this case, she was referring to her lover, Trip. He hadn't always been the patient type. Sunny had used it to her advantage back then, making Trip wait until he was almost crazy, but he had somehow learned patience over the last few months, that and other things, and it was just something else about Trip that Sunny had to learn to get used to.

Trip—Trenton Louis Hill, III—had taught her to ride, had even given her the name she now claimed like a possession. Sunny...for the glow on her wide, happy face, for the little yellow tattoo on her right asscheek, for the way he felt when she pressed that soft, tender ass up against him.

Sunny slowed, smiling smugly at the rumble and pop of her bike because no matter how many times she heard it, it still excited her, and came to a stop at the light. She nodded to her right at a twentysomething fellow with spiked yellow hair sitting and grinning at her in a red convertible. He revved his engine. She revved hers back. She could have him and five more just like him if she wanted, but these days, in the ever-present age of the cougar, Sunny found that cliché.

Sunny shook her head. It wasn't the kid's fault. Twenty years ago she would have been in his league, but this time, he had guessed wrong. Sunny blamed it on her thighs, the way they braced and held her bright yellow Harley in place.

Sunny had legs for days, and she preferred her skirts short and her shorts—like the denim ones she sported today—even shorter. She was short, barely five feet tall, but she made it count—round little ass, tight waist, and just enough tits to suit her.

But Sunny preferred her men with a little dust on them.

And it was her prerogative. She was forty-one years old and had paid her dues. She'd had the husband and the house in the burbs and she'd preferred to let the two remain a set, taking her clothes, her favorite pairs of shoes and calling it a day.

It was all a part of traveling light, and Sunny knew there was no other way to do it. Trip had known it, too. He was a loner who ran a bar across town, who had mixed her Jack and Coke like he had been doing it since creation. And now, she and Trip, they were in this life together.

Sunny blew relief from her lips as she pulled into the drive. She parked her Harley next to Trip's new sensible sedan—she wouldn't ride in that thing if you paid her—and let herself into the condo.

It didn't surprise Sunny to smell baked chicken and fresh kale when she walked in the door. Trip had traded in Chinese takeout for lessons in cooking healthy lately and Sunny was always playing the eager little guinea pig, because she was nothing if not supportive, tasting and trying his new creations. After wrapping her arms around him and squeezing Trip's middle, Sunny reached in and tore off a piece of chicken.

The breast was good, light on the butter and salt, but good. Trip swatted at her hand.

"My little speed demon...so anxious."

Trip knew Sunny well, but if it weren't for the ink that decorated his arms, neck and chest, she wouldn't recognize *him* at all, wouldn't remember that he had once been a speed demon, too, a bad boy in every sense of the word.

The heart attack had changed all that, though.

He was cooking with his shirt off, the way Sunny preferred it. When Trip turned off the stove, she ran her hands over his dark, fuzzy chest, pausing at the slick scar from his surgery.

She touched it, now a pale brown line just over his heart. Trip placed his hand over hers. He was remembering, too.

Sunny didn't like to think back to the day, but Trip wore a constant reminder of it.

It was one of the few times Sunny had ever felt fear and the only time Trip had ever seen her cry.

These days, though, Sunny denied it, said it must have been one of those mirage things Trip was having as he contemplated cascading into the light.

"We going anywhere tonight, after we eat?" Sunny asked, guiding herself back to the here and now. "There's a band playing over at Bentley's. Or did you rent a movie? Did you pick up that action flick I was telling you about?"

Trip shook his head to all. He cupped her ass inside his big hands and brought her to him, slipping, without warning, his warm tongue inside her mouth.

He said, "I thought we'd stay in. You've been going nonstop for the last three days. How about a little bit of the boob tube and off to bed?"

Trip winked and handed Sunny a freshly stirred drink.

Sunny grinned, because that, thankfully, hadn't changed about him.

And sure, it wasn't living on the edge, but it was something, she supposed, and these days Sunny took what she could get, settling on the sofa, remote in hand, sipping on a fucking perfect Jack and Coke.

There were times when Sunny didn't mind staying put, like now, when she was cuffed to their four-poster bed, facedown in a mound of pillows, sheets snatched up between her legs.

She couldn't see him, but she knew Trip was there, and these were the times Sunny paid the most attention, when she was always on edge, waiting to see what was next.

Now Trip was running pink feathers over her naked body, pausing now and then to pick up a soft leather strap to spank her eagerly twisting and waiting ass.

If she knew Trip, and she was sure she did, Sunny expected he would take advantage of how far apart her legs were spread, how wet she had become from his teasing, and take her from behind, fucking her until she whimpered, until she scratched at the sheets and bit the pillows, but Trip surprised her, leaving her dripping-wet pussy alone altogether.

Sunny was never one to protest, even though simple doggy-style would have suited her just fine. But this, this thing she felt coming, what she could feel in her bones, this was much better than doggy-style. It was better than her top three favorite positions and then some.

Sunny felt the warm tip of Trip's tongue at the rim of her ass. He had always loved her ass, had always praised and paid great attention to it. He licked her awhile, poking, prodding and lapping until she was streaming wet there, too.

"Sweet as pie," he said, and Sunny smiled, compliment whore that she was.

And then Trip crawled up behind her, his hands on either side of her arms, his heavy, thick cock swollen and throbbing against her ass and the tops of her thighs.

Trip was a well-endowed man but he had trained Sunny ever so patiently to get used to him. He eased in slow, steady, always at the absolutely perfect pace. He knew when to be gentle, knew when Sunny was ready for all of him, no holding back.

Sunny spread her legs as far as they would go. She accepted as much of him as she could stand, grunting at the pain, gushing at the pleasure. And when she felt she could take no more, Trip gave her just that, insisting, determined Sunny could take it.

Trip had such faith in her, and Sunny wanted to make him proud, so she took it all, gritting her teeth, twisting corners of the sheets until they were wet and wrinkled in her palms.

He fucked her in the ass, rhythmically stroking in and out, side to side. The weight of his body kept her pinned to the bed and she loved it.

The feeling was so good that, for the life of her, Sunny couldn't figure out what she had done to deserve it.

Had she ironed his shirts?

No.

Done the dishes when it wasn't her turn?

Definitely not.

But Sunny knew it didn't matter why. What mattered was that Trip was there fucking the life out of her until he was ready to erupt.

It never took Trip long to come when he was in her ass. It was a series of small, sweet tortures as he worked his way in, out a little, back in again. But soon he was coming, hot and furious, semen streaming between Sunny's cheeks and down her legs.

But Trip didn't forget about her, he never did. He reached beneath her and stroked her pussy with his fingers until she came, too, and Sunny lay beneath her man, pillow tucked under her chin, exhausted and sweetly sore.

And then it came.

Trip breathed the words on her neck. "I went and looked at a place today. Over in Asheville."

There it was, his ulterior motive.

Sunny could only manage a nod and Trip knew this would be so, had known all the time that when he fucked her like this, it was hard for her mind to multitask.

She soon realized Trip had planned it this way, wanted her too satiated and tired to protest.

Sunny turned over. In the brown glow of his eyes, she searched for the Trip that had been there just moments before, fucking her in the ass like a hungry beast, but that Trip was swiftly fading and was being replaced by the Trip of today, post–near death experience.

Just like a fucking woman, Trip was getting restless, wanted something simpler, something different. Wanted out of the city.

Sunny gathered her bearings enough to protest.

"I told you before, there are too many hills there to ride, Trip."

It wasn't much of an excuse, but it was the best she could do given the circumstance. Not that it even applied to Trip anymore. He hadn't pulled his bike out of the garage since the surgery, and he had been cleared for riding weeks ago.

Trip shrugged, bright eyes focused on the ceiling.

"But we could camp, hike. There's plenty we could do there."

Sunny bit on her bottom lip. "Like grow old and wrinkled. Like feel the damp weather in our brittle, tired bones. No thanks, baby."

And then there was his impatient voice. His, *I'm tired of fucking debating* voice. "It's what people our age *do*."

"Well, *some* people our age live by the philosophy, if it ain't broke..." Sunny's voice trailed off.

Sunny had gone from satisfied to pissed, from zero to a hundred and fifteen in a matter of seconds. It was always, every time, when she was distracted, when the last things on her mind were mountains and log cabins and hunting their own dinner that he brought it up and ruined everything.

It was unfair and it was frustratingly ironic.

He chose now to want to slow down. Whatever happened to living every day like it's your last? They had a good life. Luck obviously was on Trip's side. He had survived a fucking *heart attack*. Now was the time to test the waters, not rush to the shore.

Even with the heart attack and his *aha* moment, Sunny found it hard to understand. She wasn't his China doll, wasn't his tender little miss, and Trip had appreciated that once. He couldn't just turn her around like that.

"You can't keep running forever, Sunny," Trip said.

She could hear the exhaustion in his voice, and she knew that what he was saying was probably true, but for now, right now, she would run until she gave out.

Sunny threw her legs over the side of the bed.

"I'm gonna grab a shower. Them I'm going for a ride."

"A ride." Trip repeated the words as if confirming them to himself.

He shook his head, made Sunny feel like she was pathetic.

"You could come." She added it as a hopeful afterthought, a save to what was now a ruined night.

"I'll be here when you get back."

And she left him there, naked, hands locked behind his head of lion's hair and for a moment, only a moment, Sunny wondered what it might be like if maybe he wouldn't, but she quickly dismissed the thought and pulled the bathroom door closed.

She had treaded lightly long enough to let the mountain talk subside, and now Sunny was taking a misty, summer's night drive. Out of nowhere she found herself starving, yearning.

Her cunt, vibrating from the heavy hum of her bike, wanted Trip.

It would have been easy enough to wait at home for Trip, but Sunny wasn't the wait at home type, so instead she rode to the darkest part of town.

She parked in the alley behind Trip's bar and slipped in the back way.

Wearing black leather shorts and a matching corset, her beige cleavage resting over the top, Sunny eased up against Trip as he stood at the bar. She wrapped her hands around his waist, let them slide down to the front of his pants and rubbed on his bulge. Fuck whoever was watching.

The gesture didn't startle Trip at all. He knew his girl, and he had stopped being mad days ago.

He said, almost without even looking back at her, "You're gonna make me forget my orders."

Sunny shrugged and pressed her crotch against his ass, which she noted looked exceptionally hot in a pair of dark Levi's.

"So give 'em all water," Sunny said.

Trip grunted. "I think you just broke a commandment."

Sunny sucked her teeth. "Fine. Meet me in five."

Trip was there in three.

He was there in the liquor cabinet, pressing Sunny against the wall with one large hand resting on it and the other working on Sunny's zipper.

Sunny's tongue was in his mouth. She tasted remnants of bourbon. Sunny smiled at this nonconforming part of Trip's newfound conformity. She fed him continuous mouthfuls of her lips and tongue, trying her damnedest to fill the space of her recent absence.

Sunny knew how to bring it out of him, knew how to remind Trip that he, too, liked living on the edge, liked pushing until he slammed smack dab into a wall.

And then, in a flash, Sunny's shorts skidded down her legs. Trip didn't bother maneuvering her panties over her waist. He tore them off instead, discarding them on the dusty floor.

"There you go, baby," Sunny whispered, her voice low and husky, "you're still my bad boy."

Trip's velvety, dark pink lips pressed hard against hers, so hard, Sunny thought, Sunny *hoped,* they would bleed.

Sunny had learned long ago the art of productive fucking. Eight years in this thing had taught her exactly what it took to get Trip off.

In her head, Sunny recited the instructions.

Play with his balls until his cock is so hard against your palms it slaps you five. Then when he's convinced he's ready…

Sunny dropped down to her knees and wrapped her lips around Trip's cock.

Head first…he likes that…tongue around the rim…something about the sensation…fingers back on his balls…surprises and fascinates him every time even though you've done it a million...there...there...now he's begging and you don't give in and when his knees are just about ready to buckle, when his ass and thighs are trembling, when he's burgundy in the face...then you let go...demand that he save that sweet, hot come just for you...want to feel it inside of you...

As if on cue, Sunny rose. She sucked on Trip's neck awhile, then darted her tongue in and out of his ear.

"Now," she said in a voice low and hoarse, "you can fuck me. And you'd better fuck me good."

And as if the command were its own aphrodisiac, Trip's cock grew even harder as he lifted Sunny onto his haunches and backed her into the wall. It was cool on her ass.

She wrapped her pale legs around his dark ones. She grabbed tiny handfuls of his thick, coarse hair, twisted into locks that fell past his shoulders

He pushed and pushed, going deeper and deeper. Trip didn't ask Sunny if it hurt, didn't seem to really give a damn if it did.

And Sunny was wet, wet, wet at the thought of Trip not caring.

Yes, Trip, think about you right now. Think about us and this moment. The pain doesn't matter. It doesn't matter if I'm scarred or bruised. It doesn't matter if I die right here, right now, just...

"Fuck me." Sunny was hardly able to manage the words with Trip ramming her until her shoulders, back and pussy throbbed.

And just before Trip clenched his teeth, just before he was shaking again, Sunny braced her legs around him tighter, tighter than she ever had before and she covered his ever-stroking cock with her glistening orgasm.

Trip couldn't hold his own for long after that and he came, his nails clawing at her back, bringing her from the wall to his chest where she panted and said, "So, I'll see you at home, then."

Sunny was riding fast, fast, fast.

She was on a good stretch of highway, nice, long and smooth. The tar had just been redone. She could smell it.

Again, she would arrive earlier than she wanted, but it was okay. The wind felt good on her face.

She saw a curve up ahead; she liked those, liked the roller-coaster type feeling she got when she leaned down, then back up. She liked the way she lost her belly then found it again.

Then another, and it wasn't the sharpest of curves, but it caught Sunny off guard all the same and the bike leaned too far to one side.

For once, Sunny was glad she'd worn pants, tight and low-rise so at least she would look good, tough so that maybe, just maybe she could keep a little of her skin. It was the last thought that ran through Sunny's mind before she smelled burning rubber and she and the bike went down.

It didn't ache as much now, but Sunny sure didn't like the skid marks it had left on her thighs and hips. It had ruined a damn good pair of jeans, too.

But she supposed she should be grateful, should take this as her opportunity to get with that harmonious, thankful-to-be-alive shit Trip had been harping about for all these months.

He was here now, nursing her wounds, rubbing ointment on her scrapes.

"You're lucky you didn't break your hip," Trip said.

"Yeah, 'cause at my age it probably wouldn't heal worth shit," Sunny said.

"I didn't say that."

"You didn't have to."

Sunny pulled at the bristly hairs on Trip's chin. It wasn't the fall. It *absolutely* wasn't the fall. Sunny had fallen before and harder. She had broken bones and gotten back up and was back hitting the tar again within a month.

She couldn't put her finger on it, but it was something. Maybe it was the tear that Trip had furiously tried to wipe away before her eyes fluttered back open and vehemently denied even existed. Maybe it was the extralarge closet with the built-in shoe case, but suddenly, Sunny had begun hearing Asheville call her name.

She looked over at the green and gold mountain bike taking residence in a small corner of the den. It was a good day for a ride. Cool. Clear skies.

She would be breaking it in the first chance she got, and Trip, he would be right there with her on an old-man bike of his own.

Quickly, Sunny decided she would get a bell and a basket for hers, had to find some way to make the thing original. She cocked her head, eying it again. It certainly wasn't a Harley, but she knew, nonetheless, that her legs would look spectacular when she pedaled, scrapes, scars and all.

ABOUT THE AUTHORS

JACQUELINE APPLEBEE (writing-in-shadows.co.uk) has had stories in various websites and anthologies including Cleansheets, *Best Women's Erotica 2008* and *2009*, *Best Lesbian Erotica 2008*, *Tasting Him* and *Afternoon Delight*.

TENILLE BROWN's erotica is featured in various webzines and in such anthologies as *Do Not Disturb*, *Bottoms Up*, *Tasting Him*, *Iridescence*, *Naughty or Nice*, *J Is for Jealousy* and *Caught Looking*. She is a shoe and purse shopaholic and keeps a blog on her MySpace page, Myspace.com/tenillebrown.

Born in the dirty South, **CHERRY BOMB** has been performing since she was just a tiny pile of gunpowder. Conceived in the throes of a one-night stand between bell hooks and RuPaul, activism and a love of glitter are built into her sordid DNA. Catch her blogging burlesque and love at cherrybombnyc.com.

ANGELA CAPERTON's eclectic erotica spans many genres, including romance, horror, fantasy and what she calls contemporary-with-a-twist. Look for her stories published with Cleis, Circlet Press, Drollerie Press, eXtasy Books and in the indie magazine *Out of the Gutter*.

ELIZABETH COLDWELL's stories have appeared in a variety of anthologies including *Yes, Sir; Bottoms Up; Do Not Disturb* and *The Mile High Club*. This story is dedicated to anyone who has ever taken a ride in the Taxi of Shame.

ANDREA DALE's stories have appeared in *Lesbian Cowboys, The Sweetest Kiss* and *Bottoms Up*, among many others. With coauthors, she has sold two novels to Virgin Books. She thinks the Getty Villa is an amazingly sensual place. Her website is at cyvarwydd.com.

Often based on her own explorations in the world of D/s and BDSM, **TESS DANESI's** writing explores the darker side of erotica with raw honesty about that shadowy area where pain becomes pleasure and pleasure pain. She blogs at Urban Gypsy (nyc-urban-gypsy.blogspot.com) and has been published in several anthologies and *Time Out New York*.

ISABELLE GRAY's writing appears or is forthcoming in more than forty anthologies.

SUSIE HARA's work has been published (under her name as well as the pseudonym Lisa Wolfe) in *Best American Erotica 2003, Best Women's Erotica 2007, Hot Women's Erotica, Best of Best Women's Erotica* and *X: The Erotic Treasury*. Writing sexy stories is the most fun she's ever had with a laptop.

D. L. KING publishes and edits the review site, Erotica Revealed. The editor of *Where the Girls Are* and *The Sweetest Kiss*, her stories can be found in *Best Women's Erotica, Best Lesbian Erotica, Please, Ma'am* and many others. She is the author of two novels. Find her at dlkingerotica.com.

As a coed studying biochemistry and genetics, **LOLITA LOPEZ** dabbled in creating naughty tales to entertain her friends. Study for a midterm or pen a deliciously dirty story to delight her small band of fans? Not surprisingly, Lo is now on an extended sabbatical from college. She lives in Texas with her family.

KAYLA PERRIN (kaylaperrin.com) has a BA in English and sociology and a Bachelor of Education. She considered becoming a teacher—but writing was always her greatest love. She has thirty-five published works, including romance, erotica, suspense and children's fiction, and has been a *USA Today* and *Essence®* bestseller.

JENNIFER PETERS is the associate editor of *Penthouse Forum* and *Girls of Penthouse* magazines and a contributing editor to *Penthouse*. Her work has appeared in several places under numerous names, but her bylines in *Penthouse* and *Forum* are her favorites.

SUZANNE V. SLATE is a librarian who lives in the Boston area with her longtime lover. She has published a variety of nonfiction articles and a book and has recently begun writing fiction.

CHARLOTTE STEIN has a number of short stories in various erotic anthologies, including *Seduction* and *Misbehavior*. Her own collection of short stories, *The Things That Make Me Give In*, was published in 2009.

DONNA GEORGE STOREY is the author of *Amorous Woman*, a semiautobiographical tale of an American's steamy love affair with Japan. Her short fiction has appeared in numerous anthologies including *Best American Erotica*, *Best Women's Erotica*, *Bottoms Up*, *Peep Show* and *Spanked*. Read more of her work at DonnaGeorgeStorey.com.

TRISTAN TAORMINO (puckerup.com) is a writer, sex educator and pornographer. She is the author of *Opening Up: Creating and Sustaining Open Relationships*; *True Lust: Adventures in Sex, Porn and Perversion*; *Down and Dirty Sex Secrets*; *The Ultimate Guide to Anal Sex for Women* and *The Anal Sex Position Guide*.

SASKIA WALKER (saskiawalker.co.uk) is a British author whose short fiction appears in over sixty anthologies. Her erotic novels include: *Along for the Ride*, *Double Dare*, *Reckless*, *Rampant* and *Inescapable*. Saskia lives in the north of England close to the windswept Yorkshire moors, where she happily spends her days spinning yarns.

KRISTINA WRIGHT's (kristinawright.com) steamy erotica has appeared in over seventy-five anthologies, including several editions of *The Mammoth Book of Best New Erotica*; *Seduction, Liaisons and Sexy Little Numbers*; *Bedding Down: A Collection of Winter Erotica* and *Dirty Girls: Erotica for Women*. She is also the editor of *Fairy Tale Lust: Erotic Bedtime Stories for Women* (Cleis Press).

ABOUT
THE EDITOR

RACHEL KRAMER BUSSEL (rachelkramerbussel.com) is a New York–based author, editor and blogger. She is the *Best Sex Writing* series editor (bestsexwriting.com) and has edited or coedited over twenty-five books of erotica, including *Dirty Girls: Erotica for Women, Peep Show; Bottoms Up; Spanked; Naughty Spanking Stories from A to Z 1* and *2; The Mile High Club; Do Not Disturb; Tasting Him; Tasting Her; Please, Sir; Please, Ma'am; Yes, Sir; Yes, Ma'am; He's on Top; She's on Top; Caught Looking; Hide and Seek; Crossdressing; Rubber Sex; Sex and Candy; Ultimate Undies; Glamour Girls* and *Bedding Down.* She is the winner of 3 IPPY (Independent Publisher) Awards. Her work has been published in over one hundred anthologies, including *Best American Erotica 2004* and *2006*, Zane's *Chocolate Flava 2* and *Purple Panties, Everything You Know About Sex Is Wrong, Single State of the Union* and *Desire: Women Write About Wanting.* She serves as senior editor at *Penthouse*

Variations, and wrote the popular "Lusty Lady" column for the *Village Voice.*

Rachel has written for *AVN, Bust,* Cleansheets.com, *Cosmopolitan, Curve,* the Daily Beast Fresh Yarn, TheFrisky.com, Gothamist, Huffington Post, Mediabistro, *Newsday, New York Post, Penthouse, Playgirl, Radar, San Francisco Chronicle, Tango, Time Out New York* and *Zink,* among others. She has appeared on "The Martha Stewart Show," "The Berman and Berman Show," NY1, and Showtime's "Family Business." She has hosted In the Flesh Erotic Reading Series (inthefleshreading-series.com) since October 2005, which has featured everyone from Susie Bright to Zane, about which the *New York Times*'s UrbanEye newsletter said she "welcomes eroticism of all stripes, spots and textures." She blogs at lustylady.blogspot.com.